MAYBE YES

MAYBE, DEFINITELY BOOK 1

ELLA MILES

FREE BOOKS

Read **Not Sorry** for **FREE**! And sign up to get my latest releases, updates, and more goodies here→EllaMiles.com/freebooks

Follow me on BookBub to get notified of my new releases and recommendations here→Follow on BookBub Here

Join Ella's Bellas FB group for giveaways and FUN→Join Ella's Bellas Here

Want to order signed paperbacks? Visit:
store.ellamiles.com

MAYBE, DEFINITELY SERIES

Her future is already set, all she has to do is marry a complete stranger.

Kinsley Felton has everything. Money, a loving family, and a modeling career. She graduates from Yale in just days, but unlike a typical college student she doesn't have to spend hours looking for a job when she graduates. Kinsley will inherit the multi-billion dollar gaming and hospitality company her great-grandfather started. The only problem is she has to do everything her family asks for in order to get that money. That includes marrying a man of her family's choosing. That's not a problem since Kinsley has been following her family's orders all her life. Until a phone call from her grandfather changes everything.

Will she marry the man her family chooses or will she decide her own future?

MAYBE, DEFINITELY SERIES:

Maybe Yes
Maybe Never
Maybe Always

Definitely Yes
Definitely No
Definitely Forever

"WHERE THE HELL HAVE YOU BEEN?" I hear as soon as I walk into my apartment.

I smile. "Good morning."

"Don't *good morning* me! I have been worried sick and trying to fend off your father all fucking night. Where the hell were you?" Scarlett, my best friend, says.

I ignore her and walk to my closet to put my shoes back in their correct place. The closet isn't really a closet. It's more like a changing room overflowing with gifted clothes from various designers after doing shoots for them. The other half of the room is filled with every kind of makeup, jewel, and accessory I've ever worn. It's every woman's dream. I'm just not sure it's my dream.

I slip off the crop top and pull on a comfy T-shirt instead. Scarlett storms in before I've finished changing.

"Well?" she asks again. Her arms are crossed over her chest, and her foot is tapping slowly on the hard floor as she waits for my answer. Her ombre brown-colored locks flow down her back in thick curls unchanged from last night when she persuaded me to go out to a bar instead of my usual routine of hiding in my apartment to study and wait for my father to call.

"I was with Brent."

"You were with who?"

"Brent."

"I heard you the first time. You couldn't have been with a guy!"

I laugh. "Too late." Although I think I have to get further than second base to actually say I was 'with a guy.' I puked before things got too far.

"Kinsley Elizabeth Felton! You were supposed to get drunk, flirt with some guys, and then come back here with me to sleep it off—not go home with a complete stranger without telling me."

"Calm down, Scar," I say, brushing past her and heading to the kitchen to get a glass of water.

"Don't Scar me. You...you can't just..."

I laugh, seeing Scarlett so flabbergasted. She didn't think little ole me had it in me to have a one-night stand. Well, I did—sort of. I've had one boyfriend before. Scarlett is the one who dates. She's the one the guys are always after.

We are both models and both beautiful in our own right. But while I model for Seventeen magazine, Scarlett models for Victoria's Secret. I look seventeen, and she looks twenty-five. Guys find my thin frame, long legs, and blond locks attractive, but guys want to sleep with Scarlett.

It's for the best guys never want to sleep with me. I shouldn't date anyway.

I sigh. "Calm down, Scar. Nothing happened."

"What do you mean 'nothing happened'? You went home with him!"

"Yeah, well...something almost happened, but then I

threw up, and he passed out on the couch while I was in the bathroom."

Scarlett's body visibly relaxes at my words, but it doesn't stop her questions. "Why did you go home with him though?"

"I don't know." I fill my glass with filtered water. "I was drunk."

Scarlett shakes her head. "Just don't do it again."

I take a long gulp of water as I stare at Scarlett in disbelief. "You were the one who pushed me to go out."

"Yeah, and you are supposed to listen to every word I say, not go off and make your own stupid decisions like that."

I roll my eyes at her change from wild friend to motherly concern even though she has every right to be concerned. The last time I did anything remotely crazy it ended badly.

"Why are you here anyway, Scar? I thought you'd be at your apartment shooing a man out of your bed." Scarlett rarely stays over at my place. She has her own luxury apartment a block from mine. If it weren't for our parents' pocketbooks, we would have been roommates. Sometimes, I wish we had been anyway so we could have gotten the real college experience. It would have never worked though. Our clothes alone would have been too much to fit into one apartment together.

A phone vibrates, and Scarlett reaches into the pocket of her jeans. She pulls out my phone, and a worried look crosses her face. "I think you'd better answer it. Your father has been calling you nonstop, every twenty minutes, all night."

I stare at the phone, afraid to take it from Scarlett's hand. I know what's waiting for me on the other end of that phone—yelling. Lots of yelling and lecturing about my responsibilities, how immature I was last night, and how my parents should take everything away and give it to someone who will respect their terms. I can already hear my father's stern voice now.

"I'm surprised they haven't already shown up here," I say honestly. I've never missed a phone call from my father. He calls every Friday evening, and I answer instead of going out and partying with my friends. But I turned twenty-one this week. I deserved to have some fun, but now it's time to deal with the consequences.

Scarlett's eyes grow wide with fear as she thrusts the phone into my hands. "Answer it before they do show up. I don't think I could survive getting a lecture from your father."

I smile weakly as I stare at the still vibrating phone. It's not my father I have to worry about though. Our relationship has always been good. It's my grandfather's lecture that terrifies me.

"Hello?" I say, finally answering the phone. "I'm sorry I didn't answer earlier. I accidentally grabbed Scar's phone instead of mine. You know how we have the exact same phone. I was so focused on studying last night I forgot it was Friday. I fell asleep before I remembered. I'm sorry if I worried you, but I'm ready to talk now," I lie. I've never lied in my entire life. It doesn't feel natural, leaving my lips.

"Kinsley, shut up. I don't believe a word coming out of your mouth anyway. I need you to come home to Vegas immediately. I sent a jet to come pick you up," Granddad says.

"Wait...what? I have finals all next week. I need to be studying." I move my phone from my ear to make sure I saw the number correctly. It's my father's, not my grandfather's, number. *Why is my grandfather calling me on Dad's phone?*

"It's an emergency," he says grumpily into the phone. "Your father's dead."

"What?" I say, not believing his words.

He wouldn't say that to me over the phone.

"Your father's dead," he says, repeating his words. "He had a heart attack, probably due to the fact his only daughter never called him like she was supposed to. You need to come home for the funeral, and so we can decide…"

I don't hear the rest. I drop my phone and watch it clank against the hard floor. I slump to the floor. Tears stream down my face as Scarlett, my only friend, rushes to my side and holds my body in her arms.

It can't be true. It can't be.

"What happened?" Scarlett keeps asking as she holds me firmly in her arms.

"He's gone," I finally say between sobs.

And it's my fault. If I hadn't gone out last night, if I had called him, he might still be alive. If I hadn't gone out last night, I could have had one last conversation with him. I could have heard one last piece of advice. I could have heard one last 'I love you.'

I didn't though. Now, I'll never get to hear my father say those words to me again. It's all my fault. Another mistake to add to my list of flaws.

I never realized how one mistake could ruin your life.

Except, I already knew one mistake could. That was five years ago. This is nothing like that. This time, it's worse.

———

I thought the day I found out my father had died was the

worst day of my life. I thought nothing could get worse than that.

I was wrong.

I thought the funeral might be the worst day because I had to say goodbye to the only family member who had understood me at all.

I was wrong.

Today, the day after the funeral, is the worst day. Today, everything has become real. The tears are gone but not the pain. The pain is worse, much worse than I could have ever imagined. I have no one here who can comfort me or steal my mind for just a minute.

Scarlett came to Las Vegas for the funeral, but she's already gone back to Connecticut to finish her finals. She won't move back here until later this week.

My mother is a mess. We got into a fight after the funeral. It was about something petty, like what to do with the donations made in my father's honor. She can't comfort me.

And my grandfather...I wish I could stay far away from him right now.

I love my grandfather. He has done a lot for me and our family. Without him, the Felton Corporation might never have reached the heights it has. We wouldn't have more than enough money to take care of ourselves for dozens of lifetimes without even having to lift a finger. Granddad was the one who turned a simple casino into the almost twenty properties we own now. He was the one who grew the empire to what it is today.

He has given me direction in my life. He was the one who got me the modeling jobs. He was the one who decided I should go to Yale. He was the one who decided I should major in theater. He was the one who chose my whole future.

And I know why he has brought me here—to decide what comes next.

I'm usually thankful for his guidance. He's always right. He's even right about what he's brought me here to tell me. I'm just not prepared to hear it yet. I'm not ready to hear it on the worst day of my life. Today, I need to go back downstairs and finish watching the Harry Potter marathon and drown in a tub of buttered popcorn. I need to feel sorry for myself. I need to feel angry with the world. I don't need to deal with this.

"Take a seat, princess," Granddad says, indicating for me to take a seat opposite him.

But I can't. I'm frozen in the doorway. He called me princess. Only my father ever called me that.

Tears I didn't even know still existed threaten to fall as my eyes fill with moisture. I thought I had cried all the tears out.

Granddad immediately realizes his mistake. His arms are quickly around me in a hug, but it doesn't stave off the tears. They fall fast and hard. My body moves from a frozen statue into uncontrollable trembles. I feel my grandfather guide me over to a chair. My body collapses into the chair, but it doesn't stop the trembling or the tears.

He hands me a handkerchief before moving back to his seat across from me. I wipe my eyes, and then I stare at him. Nobody would know he is eighty-five years old. He looks sixty, tops. It's the lucky Felton genes. He doesn't work out or eat any better than I do.

"We need to talk about your future."

I nod, expecting this.

"We need to figure out who is going to run the company in your father's place."

I nod again.

"As you already know, your father and I argued a lot. We never agreed on anything." He sits back in his chair, smiling a little at a memory.

When he looks back at me, he frowns. He thinks I'm the reason his son is dead. I don't think he'll ever forgive me.

Maybe he would if I gave him everything he ever wanted?

"But we did agree on one thing," he continues.

I already know what that one thing is.

"That you want the company to stay in the family," I say, completing his sentence.

His frown deepens. "Yes. Your mother isn't capable of running the company. And, frankly, neither are you."

Now, it's my turn to grimace. Although I already knew how he felt, it hurts to hear my father felt the same way. He didn't have any more confidence in my abilities than my grandfather did. It stings I was never even considered for the job even though I'm family. I'm the only heir to the empire.

"We all agreed the best thing for the company is for you to marry someone who *is* capable of running the company —a man your father and I would choose after years of scrutiny."

I nod. I already knew all of this. It's why I never really dated. It doesn't matter whom I want to be with. It only matters who is best for the company. I'll marry for my family, not for love.

It's always been years into the future though. I'm only twenty-one. I haven't even officially graduated yet. I haven't even met the guys my father and grandfather have been considering. I haven't tested out the men myself to at least make sure whomever they might choose would be a good fit.

"Well..." Granddad pauses like it's hard for him to say the next words because he knows how much I'll hate them. "We found him."

My mouth falls open. I wasn't expecting that. I didn't know he and my father had already chosen a man for me. I thought I still had time left.

"You'll meet him tomorrow."

I nod. It's all I can do.

"And then you'll marry him in six months."

My eyes grow wide at his words. *Six months?* I can't marry someone I've never met in six months. I don't even know if I'll be able to tell if I like the guy in six months. I won't even be over mourning my father in that amount of time.

"I can't..." I whisper. The words feel strange falling from my mouth. I don't think I've ever said those words to any member of my family, even my mother. I've always been the good girl following their every order. I've always been their princess who never disobeys. Right now, I don't know if I can ever be that girl again.

Granddad walks over to me and rests his hand on my shoulder. It's meant to be comforting, except it's not.

I can't get married in six months. I just can't. A few years, maybe. That was always the plan—do the modeling and acting thing for a little longer, and then in my late twenties, they would match me with a guy who they felt was capable of running the company but would also be a good match for me. We would date like a normal couple and then marry by the time we were thirty.

I'm only twenty-one. That's nowhere near thirty. And I

can't focus on anything right now except my father being gone.

"Oh, sweetie, you can."

I incredulously stare up at him. I don't know how he can focus on anything except his son being gone right now, but I guess the company comes first. It always comes first.

"I...I don't think so." My eyes beg for him to change his mind, to understand I'm not ready to get married. I don't even know who I am yet or what I want in life.

"I'm sorry. I know we all wanted to wait until you were older, but it's time. I'm not getting any younger. I need to know the company is in the right hands before I go."

I tuck my long strands behind my ear. I can't believe he is talking about his death right now. I nervously run my hands through my hair over and over.

"I'm not ready," I say without meeting his eyes. I can't face disappointing him again.

"Yes, you are. You're beautiful. You were born to marry a man who can run the Felton empire. Once you are married, you will see it was the right thing to do. You will feel taken care of. You will finally feel like you have found your place in this world."

I let my eyes glance up at him for just a second. I see honesty. His eyes are filled with honesty.

"Maybe," I say weakly.

His face brightens. "Yes," he says.

"Yes," I repeat on autopilot.

"The meeting is tomorrow at eleven a.m. at the Felton Grand on the strip."

"Yes," I say again. I stand up without looking him in the eyes. I walk out of the door without looking back.

I walk back to the basement, back to my haven. This time, when I slump into the chair, I don't feel an ounce of comfort. In fact, I feel nothing. Sitting here and watching movies the rest of the day isn't going to help anymore. I won't be able to zone out on them again. I just promised my grandfather I would marry a total stranger in six months. I've never broken a promise before, and I don't plan on starting now.

I just don't know what I want.

I think of everything I've been told I want—money, clothes, a modeling career, an acting career, and an intelligent husband who will run our company to give me even more money. But not one of those things has ever made me happy. I try to think about things that have made me happy —my family and Scarlett. But that leaves me with fewer answers.

I know what I don't want.

I don't want a modeling career.

I don't want an acting career.

I don't want to marry a complete stranger.

I try to think of my happiest memory with my dad. It was on my eighteenth birthday. It coincided with my high school graduation. He took me to a casino in California, one I could legally gamble at. He taught me how to play blackjack and how to count cards. We won—a lot. It wasn't the winning that made it fun. It was learning something from my father. It was the confidence he displayed in me when he gave me high amounts of money to place a bet I would win because I was capable. It was one of the only times I felt he was proud of me for something other than my looks.

The line I will never forget my father saying to me is, "No one would ever suspect you of counting cards. You're too pretty."

It was that day I learned my beauty was a weapon I

could use to my advantage. I just never learned how to harness it.

I head to my room to grab my shoes and purse to head to a casino, to find a happy memory...because tomorrow I'll meet the man I'm going to marry. Tomorrow I'll have to face the fact I don't get to decide my future. I don't have to face it today though. I still have a chance to make today better.

I was wrong. Today isn't the worst day of my life either. Tomorrow probably will be, so I'm going to make the most of my last night of freedom.

2

I PLACE five hundred dollars in chips on the table—my maximum bid. The true count is up to plus-six, so I need to bet high since a positive true count tells me I have an advantage over the dealer. I watch as the dealer deals out the cards. In my head, I silently keep track of the cards being laid out. I look at my cards—a jack and a ten. I smile at the twenty, just one short of twenty-one—the number I want to match without going over. The dealer turns to me on my turn, and I signal I want to stand.

I watch the dealer flop an additional card to add to his fifteen. It's a king. He's busted at twenty-five. I smile as he hands me a thousand dollars in additional chips bringing my winnings up to five thousand for the night.

I should stop soon. Not stopping is always the chance you take when you play against the house. The house always has the advantage, even when you count cards, even when you know the odds. There is always a chance you will lose the hand, you will lose track of the count, or you will get cocky and bet too much.

But I didn't come here to win. Although winning feels good, I came here to escape. So, I'll keep playing, no matter what.

"You're good. You should teach this old man to play. I'm having terrible luck," an older gentleman sitting next to me says.

I smile at the sweet old man. He's been sitting next to me for over an hour now, and I don't think he's won more than a couple of hands. He is down well over a thousand dollars.

I bid my maximum five hundred again. I keep my eyes on the cards as the dealer deals. I silently keep up the running count while still giving attention to the older gentleman.

"It's just beginner's luck. I haven't played in years."

The man smiles at me. "It looks like more than luck to me."

I shake my head as I smile back. I watch as the man takes his turn. He has seventeen. He should stand. If he hits, there is a good chance he will bust. He hits and busts. I knowingly shake my head.

It's my turn. I get a blackjack. I smile as the dealer pushes more chips my way.

The old man sitting next to me shakes his head in disbelief of my winning streak. I try to act innocent by twirling the long blond hair of my high ponytail with my fingers. I don't want to draw attention to my card counting, not that anyone would expect a young woman in jeans, a ripped comfy sweatshirt, and no makeup to be counting cards. But if security does catch on, I know enough about casinos to know I'll be kicked out.

I silently divide the running count by the decks left in the shoe. I get negative four indicating I'm at a disadvantage. I place a low bet this time, expecting to lose. I do.

"Guess my winning streak can't last forever."

The older gentleman chuckles. "Maybe your luck has passed to me."

I glance up from the table when I see them—the most intense eyes I have ever seen. The eyes belong to a man in a suit. The kind of man who knows designer clothes and only wears the best. A man that demands attention wherever he walks because of his mere presence. The kind who spends all day in a boardroom but still looks like he spends all of his time at the gym. I can't believe I haven't noticed him before. I've been sitting at this table for over an hour. In that time, many people have come and gone. None of them were the least bit intriguing.

There is something about the way this man is looking at me that sends goosebumps all over my body. I'm not sure what the look actually is. *Is it lust? Interest? Anger? Frustration?* I don't know. All I can feel is the intensity of his eyes. And they are staring at me. His eyes don't leave me as the dealer begins dealing.

I glance back at the table to continue counting the cards, but I still feel his eyes burning into me. I lose track of the count, not really caring anymore. I hit even though I'm at nineteen, and it doesn't make sense. I bust.

"I think I've pushed my luck too far at this table. Good luck," I say to the older gentleman next to me. I stand from the table, taking my chips with me.

I make it a point to avoid looking at the man in the suit with the intense eyes, but I still feel his eyes on me. I'm not ready to leave yet. As soon as I leave, my world will no longer be in my control—*not that it ever was in my control.* I need more of a distraction.

I walk to the bar in the center of the casino and take a seat. I relax as my butt hits the cushion of the barstool. I know I can't sit here for long without ordering a drink, which is the last thing I want. Maybe I'll try my hand at pushing the buttons on the slots. I know I'll end up losing all the money I just won, but I don't care.

"So, you're a pro."

"What?" I turn left, toward the direction of the voice.

That's when I see them—the same piercing eyes. It's the same man who was watching me at the blackjack table.

I flip the chips over in my hands at the bar.

"A pro card counter," he says as he takes a seat next to me.

Shit. I'm about to get thrown out of here.

"I don't know what you're talking about." I turn back to the bar. I try to get the attention of one of the scantily clad bartenders, but the closest one to me is busy flirting with a man.

Out of the corner of my eye, I watch my visitor as he raises his hand, and the bartender immediately smiles and begins walking over to us.

"Yes, you do. Don't worry. I'm not going to turn you in."

I exhale a breath I didn't even know I had been holding. "Do you work here?"

"No."

I don't know how to respond to that, so I don't. I have no idea why this complete stranger followed me. It's not like the other night at the bar when I was dressed to pick up a guy. Tonight I look like death. No one is attracted to that. So, he can't be here to hook up with me. He's not here to kick me out. That leaves...I have no idea.

"What can I getcha?" The woman leans over the bar, pushing her cleavage closer to the man's face.

I watch his lips move, but I don't register his words. He

doesn't ask me what I want. He just speaks to the bartender, while keeping his eyes on me.

I stupidly assumed his eyes would be on the pair of boobs in front of him giving me an opportunity to check him out. I was wrong.

Now, I can't take my eyes off of him even though my cheeks are burning red with embarrassment. I notice his suit conforms to his body, making it obvious he doesn't work here. His dark brown hair spikes slightly to one side, and I think there is a little red in it if I look closely. He has a hint of a five o'clock shadow outlining his downturned lips that seem just as intense as his eyes.

The whole time I'm taking him in, he doesn't move. His expression never changes. I'm used to men at least smiling at me, but his lips don't curl upward even a hint.

He's older. I know that much. He has lines around his eyes that hint at him being older than me. I have no idea how much older though—maybe ten years, if I had to guess. Closer to thirty than twenty.

He's intimidating.

His eyes don't shift from mine until the bartender returns with our drinks, and he reaches into his pocket to hand the woman his shiny platinum credit card.

I glance at the bar and see two glasses of wine sitting in front of us. The bartender returns his credit card having opened his tab.

"Thanks," I say.

He nods and takes a sip of his wine. I do the same. As soon as the liquid touches my lips, my whole attitude toward this stranger changes. The liquid is exquisite. No, it's better than exquisite. It's the best thing I've ever tasted. It puts the Cosmo my almost one night stand got me the other night to shame.

"This is delicious." I hold up the wine to my lips and take another sip.

"Good," he says, seeming satisfied with my response.

I curiously look at him. "Why are you here?"

"Because I'm like every other person on the planet who likes to drink and occasionally gamble his money away while looking at boobs."

I smile bashfully when he says 'boobs' even though he isn't talking about mine. Mine are completely covered up, if you can even call what I have boobs.

He, on the other hand, still hasn't cracked a smile.

"I meant..." I shake my head. I'm not going to ask.

"I'm intrigued by you. You're beautiful, yet I detect a bit of insecurity in you for reasons that don't make sense. You are obviously intelligent if you are able to count cards, but you are used to your beauty helping you to cover up that intelligence, just like you did with your card counting. You seem sad, yet you've chosen to come to one of the most alive places on the planet. You have every reason to be confident, yet you act like a scared, innocent little girl. I'm just trying to figure out what *you* are doing here."

I narrow my eyes at his rude comments. *How could he have formed such a strong opinion of me in such a short amount of time?* "Thank you for the drink," I say as I stand. I'm not going to sit here and listen to a stranger insult me, not tonight.

He grabs my arm as I get up. "I didn't mean that as criticism."

"Seemed like it to me," I say cautiously as I stare at his hand holding my arm. I feel the heat transfer from his body to mine. It feels overpowering, like everything else coming from this man.

"Let's try again. I'm Killian. You seem like a nice woman.

I would love to hear over another drink how you became so good at blackjack and hopefully get some tips because I sucked back there." This time, after he speaks, his lips curl up slightly.

It's not quite a smile, but I can tell it's pushing it for this man.

I smile brightly, hoping that if I smile, he will too.

"I'm Kinsley," I say, extending my hand and returning to my seat.

Killian shakes it like it's a business arrangement. I suck in my breath at his touch. His handshake is powerful and strong. It's practiced, like he has shaken a million hands. I bet he can close business deals with just the strength of his handshake.

"And I would love more wine." I take another sip of my wine, finishing it off.

He nods to the bartender this time, and she immediately comes over to him even though the bar is now full, and it's not our turn to be served.

"Another?" the woman asks him, smiling brightly.

He nods.

She winks at him before she goes to retrieve our drinks.

My mouth stays open. "How did you do that?"

He raises an eyebrow. "Order drinks?"

"How did you get her attention like that? Are you a regular or something?"

"No. Bartenders just know where their biggest tip lies. And that's with me."

I nod although I'm not sure if that's completely it. He definitely has the sex-appeal thing going for him. And the intense almost lust-filled look he gives would make any woman say yes immediately.

I find myself wondering what it would be like if he

asked me to go home with him tonight. *How different would it be from Brent, my almost one night stand from hell?* I shake my head, getting that thought out of my head. I can't have sex with this man—not that he is asking me anyway.

The bartender places our drinks in front of us. I immediately grab the glass and bring it to my lips to taste the sweet, smooth liquid again. I moan quietly as the liquid pours down my throat. The taste is magical. I've never had anything like it.

"My father."

His eyes find mine, but he doesn't say a word.

"My father taught me how to play blackjack."

He nods.

"He taught me how to count cards." My cheeks flush slightly from my admission.

I think I see a hint of a smile forming, but I don't know how to keep that smile on his lips. I don't know how to flirt and show him I need a distraction.

"He passed away..." I blurt out, but can't add that he died this week. Then, I wait. I wait for the *I'm sorry*. I wait for the *Is there anything I can do for you?* I wait for the *How are you doing?*

"Let's get out of here."

My eyes widen. "What?"

"We are leaving." Killian stands from his seat, throws a hundred dollar bill on the bar as a tip, and begins walking in the direction of the exit.

I laugh. *He's got to be kidding.*

When I glance at him, I realize he's not. His face is stoic as he waits just a couple feet from me to follow him.

"What?"

"This isn't what you need."

I laugh again before I glance back up at his eyes. "How do you know what I need?"

Killian walks to me until his body just grazes mine. His eyes stay on mine as his hand tucks my hair behind my ear. His hand doesn't stop there though. It trails down my neck as he pushes my hair back until he is gently holding the nape of my neck. My breath catches. Shivers form all over my body. An ache for more forms in my belly, but I don't let my need show. A complete stranger can't turn me on this much. It took Brent most of the night to get me this filled with lust. *How has this stranger done it with barely a touch?*

I watch as he bends down. For a second, I think he's going to kiss me, but he doesn't. Instead, his lips move inches away from my neck so I can feel his hot breath there. I can't move. I can't breathe.

"Your body tells me. Your eyes are begging me to kiss you," he whispers into my ear. His deep voice causes fluid to soak my panties. "You're wet."

I suck in a breath, proving him right.

"You want me to take you to my hotel room down the strip and fuck you until you scream." He moves away from my neck. "That's what you need."

He cocks his head and grins for the first time. It's a beautiful sight, and it's a side of him I doubt he displays often.

I nod, and he smiles brighter.

"Come," he says, holding his hand out to me.

I blush at the double meaning of the word. I bite my lip as I debate on what to do. I reach for the phone in my pocket, but I let my hand fall to my side. My father isn't here to guide me. Scarlett can't give me any advice. I have to decide this one on my own. And my body is begging me to go with this stranger. I have no doubt he will know how to handle my body.

But I can't. I tried it once, and I ended up puking alone in a stranger's bathroom while my father was dying.

"I ca—"

His lips stop me from speaking as his tongue slips into my mouth in one motion. The kiss is long and slow. His tongue takes complete control as he explores my mouth. Owning my tongue with complete authority. When he breaks from the kiss, I'm panting, unable to catch my breath.

"Come with me. You need this."

I stare at him, still panting hard, while I try to decide if he is a serial killer or not. Based on that kiss though, I'm not sure if I care. I would die happy, kissing this man.

I grab my glass of wine and down the last few drops, hoping the liquid will calm my nerves. It does.

"At least let me take you to get another bottle of your favorite wine."

"It's not my favorite."

"Yes, it is."

I turn back to the bar, expecting him to order another glass of wine.

"They're all out."

"I doubt it." I try to flag down the bartender, but she won't stop for me. I sigh.

"Don't trust me?"

"No, I don't."

He flags her down. "Another round," he says without glancing at her breasts.

"I'm sorry, sir. We are all out of that wine. Can I recommend another one?"

"No, thank you, Clarissa."

My eyes grow wide at the mention of the bartender's

name. Her name tag sits across the left side of her blouse just above her cleavage. So, he did check out her tits.

"Come split a bottle of wine with me."

"Maybe," I say. I can't help but smile. I need this. I need to have one night to sleep with whomever I want before I never get to choose again. I need to finish what I never got with my last attempt at a one night stand.

"I'll take that as a yes."

———

3

Killian's hotel room is impressive. It's one of the most impressive hotel rooms I've been in, and I've been in a lot. It's large and spacious, and has more rooms than any hotel room should. It's also in the Felton Grand, one of my family's hotels. I didn't want to come here yet. Not so soon after my father passed away. Not when this is the place I would miss him the most. But I didn't want to tell Killian the truth when he brought me to this hotel, so I came.

I shake nervously on the couch as I watch him pour two glasses of wine. The nerves at least keep me from thinking about my father. He hands me my glass of wine, and he takes his and sits in a chair opposite to me. I hate that he is sitting there. I want him to sit next to me. I want him to kiss me. I want him to sleep with me, like he promised.

Instead, he sits, patiently watching me, as we both sip our wines.

"What do you do?" I ask, trying to distract my nerves.

"Do you really want to know? Or would you prefer, when I make you come, you don't know anything about me?

That way, when this is over, you can go back to whatever you are running from without any attachment."

"How do you know I'm running from something? Maybe I'm just missing my father."

"You are."

I just nod. I don't know if he means, I'm running from something, missing my father, or both.

"What about you? What do you do?"

"I thought we weren't going to talk specifics."

"No. I'm not going to tell you about me. The more you know, the more it's likely that you will get attached."

God, why am I here when this man keeps insulting me? I frown. "I won't get attached."

"No?" He raises his eyebrows.

Killian's probably right. If I fall for him, it will only give me more of a reason to run from whomever my father and grandfather have chosen for me.

"Fine." I sigh. "But I don't want to tell you about me either."

If I don't get to know anything about this man, he doesn't get to know anything about me.

He nods and takes a slow sip of his drink.

"When are we going to..." my voice says shakily.

"Fuck?" he says, finishing my sentence.

Wine slips from my mouth at how easily the word rolled off his tongue. He probably says *fuck* daily. He probably fucks daily. *I'm never going to live up to the women he's had before.* I try to push that thought out of my head. *He chose me.* And he doesn't have to know how inexperienced I am.

"Come here," he says, motioning for me to come to him.

I place my glass on the coffee table and walk to him. When I reach him, he remains seated. So, I stand awkwardly in front of him. I fidget with my hands, not sure what he wants me to do.

Killian chuckles in a deep raspy voice, like he hasn't used his voice to laugh in a long time. His hand grabs my wrist, and he pulls me hard onto his lap.

He strokes my cheek. "Don't think, princess."

I try to listen to his words. I try not to think as his mouth kisses down my neck, leaving warm, wet tingles. I can't help the tears that begin welling in my eyes. Of all the terms of endearment he could have chosen to use, I can't believe he chose the one that reminds me of my father, the one nickname my father always used to call me.

When he sees my tears, he softly kisses them with his lips before licking up the salty liquid with his tongue.

"What's wrong, princess? We don't have to do this." He tucks my hair back behind my ear before his hand softly rubs my back. "I just thought you might need it."

"Why did you call me princess?"

He smiles weakly at me. "Because you are one."

"What do you mean?"

"You're beautiful." He softly kisses my hand. "You're intelligent." He kisses my other hand. "You're used to being taken care of." He softly kisses me on the cheek. "You're a little too sweet and naive." He kisses the other cheek. "Your clothes are simple yet expensive." His kiss brushes softly on my lips. "You should be worshipped." He runs a hand through my hair. "You're a princess in every sense of the word."

I smile at how intuitive he is. He's picked up a lot about me in the short amount of time we have been together.

"Okay."

"Okay?"

"Okay, you can call me princess."

He wipes my remaining tears on my cheeks. "It's going to be okay, princess."

I suck in a breath as he grabs the nape of my neck and kisses me hard on the lips. I moan as his tongue massages mine. His kisses are deep and intense. His kisses are full of purpose.

I hold on to his neck as he kisses me. I'm too unsure of what to do with my hands to do much else, even though my hands are desperate to rip off his suit jacket and buttoned-down shirt to see what lies beneath them.

Instead, he lifts me and carries me to a room with a lavish bed covered in throw pillows. I land softly among the pillows. I watch as he removes his jacket and carefully places it over the back of a chair in the corner of the room. He removes his tie before he unbuttons the top couple of buttons of his shirt.

I watch as he climbs over me, but his body doesn't touch mine. My heart pounds erratically in my chest as I stare up at the thick, muscle of a man above me. I squeeze my hands into fists to prevent myself from running my hands all over his body.

Killian squints his eyes at me before he takes my hand and presses it against his chest. "You can touch." He smirks at me.

He leans down and kisses me again, hard. It's so forceful he sucks all the air from my chest. His hand slides up my shirt, massaging the exposed skin of my stomach. His eyes occasionally open to study my reaction when he takes everything a step further, but he doesn't slow down or hesitate. The intensity of his stare is there every time he opens his eyes. I can't help but keep my eyes open, needing to take in every moment of this man.

I let my hand slip into the opening of his shirt to feel his hard chest, but I don't let myself explore beyond that. His hand mimics mine, except his moves with more confidence and surety. I gasp when his hand expertly finds my nipple beneath my shirt. He slowly rubs the peak between his thumb and finger.

"Don't think, princess. Just feel," he whispers into my ear.

This time, I do what he says. All I feel is the intensity building inside me. He releases my lips, and his tongue discovers my other nipple as he lifts my shirt up.

"Oh, wow," I moan when he flicks his tongue.

"You're beautiful, princess."

His words barely register. I can't focus on anything but the sensations on my breasts.

His hand slips down my pants, and my heart rate increases in anticipation. He takes my pants off in one fluid motion, and then I'm exposed. My shirt is lifted high above my breasts, and my pants now lie in a pile on the floor while Killian is still completely clothed. *Why the hell is he still clothed?*

When his mouth sinks lower until his tongue touches my clit, I no longer care he is still clothed. All I care about is that he keeps doing that.

"Oh my god!" I moan louder than I probably should.

I feel his mouth curl into a smile, but his tongue never leaves my clit.

"God, don't ever stop whatever the hell you are doing." I breathe fast as he swirls his tongue faster and faster over my bud.

When he sticks two fingers inside me, I almost lose it.

"Killian!" I scream as he stretches me.

The sensation is beyond words. His fingers seem to fill

me completely. I can't imagine how it will feel to have his cock pushed deep inside me.

His fingers move faster inside me as his tongue moves in rhythm with them.

"Come for me," he commands in between thrusts inside me.

"Oh, fuck," I moan as I come, just like he commanded.

His fingers slowly and reluctantly move out of me, but I can't move. I'm too exhausted.

I just came on a man's fingers while his mouth tasted my juices. That's a first. I've had sex before, sure, but no man has ever made me come before. Maybe that's why I never went to seek it out. If I knew orgasms could feel better than the ones I give myself with a vibrator, I would have sought out men who could give orgasms like Killian sooner. I wonder if he is as good at making a woman orgasm when he's thrusting deep inside her.

"Be right back, princess," he says. He gently kisses my lips. It's a stark contrast to the kisses he was giving me just moments earlier.

I exhale deeply for the first time in a long time as I sink into the bed. I close my eyes as I wait for him to come back. I don't bother with covering my naked body. Modeling has taught me not to be shy about my body, and I want more.

When Killian comes back, I'll be brave. I'll show him what I want. I want him to fuck me like I'm sure he has with countless women before. I want to feel slutty and dirty. I want to feel wild. For the first time in my life, I want to fuck a complete stranger.

4

―――――

I WAKE up suddenly as I'm thrown from another nightmare about my father's death. I try to wipe the tears streaming down my cheeks, but I can't move. I'm pinned to the hotel bed by a hot stranger's arm.

His arm feels nice, stretched across my body—that is, until I realize we are both naked. Completely naked. Not I'm-wearing-underwear-and-a-bra kind of naked. No, I'm utterly naked. He is, too. I know because his leg is draped over me, and his erection is pressed against my hip.

I lie in the bed, frozen, not sure what to do. I don't want to wake him, but I can't stay here in bed all day although it does feel good to be wrapped in a hot stranger's arms.

I know how this goes though. As soon as he wakes up, I'll awkwardly try to get dressed while he tries to find the best way to kick me out as fast as possible. I can't handle that—not today, not ever.

Maybe if I just slowly slip off the bed, I can get out, get dressed, and escape the hotel room before he even wakes up to avoid the tension bound to happen if he wakes up. Then, I can go back to my own bed and forget this ever happened. Except, after a night like last night, I don't know if I'll ever be able to forget. I've never orgasmed so hard in my life. My only regret is not actually having sex. I have no idea why Killian is naked.

I gently begin moving his arm off my chest, already feeling the cold the second his arm falls to the bed. I wince, afraid he is going to wake up, but he doesn't. I run my fingers harshly across my cheeks, flinging the tears from my face. Now, I just have to get out from beneath his muscular leg. I try to shimmy off the bed, but I can't. His leg is holding me in place. I try lifting—

"What are you doing, princess?"

I glance over at Killian. His eyes are still shut, and his five o'clock shadow has grown slightly overnight.

"Um..." I swallow hard. "I need to pee, and I have a meeting in five hours I need to get to."

Killian leans over and softly kisses me on the lips. "I'll order breakfast then."

He moves off of me and gets out of bed. I watch his bare ass as he walks to his suitcase. He pulls out a pair of jeans and slips them on without putting underwear on first. I curiously look at this man. His body is even better than I imagined, his muscles are sculpted into thick strands of hard steel along his back down to his cute butt I want to squeeze. I just wish I could have seen the front of his body.

He leaves me alone in the bed.

Weird. My experience after my almost one-night stand is that the guy wants you out fast. If not that, then I would assume he would be looking for sex. But Killian did neither of those things. *Maybe he doesn't find me attractive?*

I shake my head. *It doesn't matter what he thinks. Today will be the last day I ever see him,* but it still stings. It hurts that he doesn't even want to have sex with me.

I get dressed quickly, but linger in the bedroom because I'm embarrassed. He has seen me naked and done untold things to my body while I barely even touched his.

Maybe he wanted a blow job, and I didn't even offer?

Maybe he has a girlfriend?

Maybe he was drunker than I thought and has a hangover?

Maybe he's into guys?

When I hear the door to the hotel room open and shut, followed closely by the smell of bacon, I can't hide out in the bedroom any longer. My stomach rumbles loudly as I open the door.

Killian, still shirtless, is pouring coffee at the small table in the dining room. He stops and looks at me as I enter the room. He doesn't smile. He doesn't have to. His eyes say everything—that he's attracted to me, that he wishes I were naked again and back in bed—but something is holding him back from doing what he really wants. I wish I knew what that was.

I let my eyes drop to his body as I make my way over to the table that is large for a hotel room, even for a suite. From the looks of his muscles, it's obvious he works out but not in the obsessed-with-the-gym sort of way, simply in the I-care-about-my-body-and-want-to-be-healthy-and-look-good sort of way.

My mouth is gaping, I realize, as I stare at his body. "I, uh...your body...you look good," I say, trying to make up for why I'm gawking awkwardly at him.

He chuckles at my broken words. I quickly bite my lip to keep it from falling open again and saying anything more embarrassing.

"I didn't know what you would want for breakfast, so I ordered two options. There is a healthy option or an I-want-to-die-happy option."

I take a seat opposite him and grab the plate with the pancake, eggs, and bacon before I change my mind. His eyes grow wide, but he doesn't say anything.

I smile. "It wasn't what you thought I would choose?" I slightly raise my eyebrows, waiting for him to respond.

Killian frowns, shaking his head. "No."

That's when I look at the plate in front of him. A majority of the plate is fruit and vegetables along with an egg white omelet. He's not drinking coffee, only water. He's a health nut. Maybe I shouldn't have shown my true colors in front of him, but I don't really care. After breakfast, I will never see this man again.

"How are you feeling this morning?"

I bite into my pancake, the food immediately settling my stomach.

"Hungry," I say.

I dig more into my meal so I don't have to talk. I don't know what you are supposed to say when having breakfast with a man you almost had sex with. And he doesn't seem like a huge talker anyway. So, maybe he will enjoy the silence.

"When did your father die?"

I was wrong. He's a talker. I stare awkwardly up at this stranger, not sure I want to confide in him. *But I need to confide in someone, so why not him?* He's already told me he doesn't want me to get attached, so he's not looking for anything beyond whatever happens this morning.

"He died four days ago." I don't look at him. I just shovel more food into my mouth.

"That's what I thought," he says, his voice sounds sad, withdrawn. "Were you close?"

"Yes, he was the only person in my family who even remotely understood me."

"I'm sorry," he says after a long pause.

I give him a weak smile as I glance up from my food. He seems genuine. I nod, but words like that never make me feel any better, no matter how genuine they are.

A few seconds pass as we both make huge dents in our breakfast plates. Neither of us speak. I barely even breathe.

"I've never lost anyone like that. I can't imagine the pain you are going through..."

"It's not something I ever thought I would go through. And I'm not sure how I'm going to get through it right now. The pain is unbearable. I know I have to find a way...for him."

He nods and waits for me to say more, but I don't.

"His death is what you're running from," he says.

I stare off into the distance. *Is that what I'm running from? His death?* I think for a moment. *No, it's not his death I'm running from. It's my future.*

"No," I say firmly. "I'm running from family obligations that have been sped up now that he's gone."

His mouth turns upward into a slight smile. I have no idea why my statement would make a man who hardly ever smiles, smile.

"Now, that's something I can understand."

I run my hands through my hair, trying to read into that sentence's meaning. *What family obligations could a man almost in his thirties have?* He can't still be following his parents' orders, like I am. That could only mean one thing...

"Oh my God! You're married, aren't you? You probably have four or five kids at home you're responsible for." I push away from the table and begin searching the hotel room for my purse, but I don't see it. *Shit*, I silently curse. I'll have to leave and get a new ID and credit cards later. I don't care about the cash I will lose. It's not worth staying around to find out I was the other woman—even if it was only for one night.

"Whoa...slow down there, princess." He grabs my arm so I can't move. "I'm not married," he says slowly, like if he talks slower, it will somehow make his words more believable. "And I sure as hell don't have four or five kids."

He cocks his head to the side, like he thinks I'm crazy. Maybe I am. I swallow hard, watching his desire grow in his eyes as he looks at me.

"You're not married?" I ask hesitantly.

"No," he says, smirking at me.

"You don't have kids?"

"No."

I stare at his lips until they move so close to mine that I can barely breathe. His hands move up to tuck my blond hair behind my ear. I shiver at his touch. He doesn't kiss me though. He just hovers, obviously wanting more but denying himself what he wants for some reason.

I don't know what comes over me. I don't know if it's the fact that this man has already kissed me, and I already miss his lips. I don't know if it's the fact his desire for me is so obvious I can basically feel his heart beating fast beneath his chest because of me. I don't know if it's because today is the last day I get to choose who I can and can't kiss.

Whatever the reason, I kiss him. I grab his neck as I do, so he can't pull away. My kiss is defiant and carnal. It's wet and deep and everything a kiss should be—except this time, when I kiss him, he barely kisses me back. *Maybe I'm doing it wrong?* But I know I'm not. I can feel his erection growing as it presses into my stomach. So, I don't stop.

It only takes a few seconds more until he is kissing me back with as much hunger as he was before. I smile against his lips as he does. Maybe we will be having sex after all.

Our kisses quicken as we both become more and more desperate for more, for unfulfilled promises from last night. We stumble backward until my body is trapped between him and a wall behind me. It feels nice to be possessed in such a way. When he lifts my body, I wrap my legs around his waist and moan because it's exactly what I wanted him to do.

I don't stop kissing him as he carries me back to the bedroom. I don't stop until he roughly throws me onto the bed.

I smile as he stares at me with those intense eyes that say so much when his mouth doesn't. I watch as they turn from lust-filled to empty. I run my tongue over my lip, trying to look sexy, but the moment has passed, and I have no idea why.

"You should go," he says.

My eyes widen, but I don't ask why. I'm not going to beg someone to sleep with me when he obviously doesn't want to.

"Okay, help me find my purse." I must look disappointed as I stand and gather myself from the bed.

"Don't. Don't think that. I want you. I'm desperate for you..." He looks down. "I just can't. I'm not going to be the guy you lose yourself in because you are running away. When I fuck you, it will be because you want me as much as I want you right now."

I laugh nervously. "I thought we were done after today."

He looks at me even more seriously, if that is possible. "No. Today is the beginning."

I try to smile, but I can't. This man is insane. No, he's bipolar. One minute, he can't keep his hands off of me, and the next, he's a knight in shining armor. I just wish I knew which was a facade and which was the real Killian.

I walk out of the bedroom and back into the living area. I hear Killian following me, but I don't turn to face him. I just walk.

"Here," he says, holding out my purse.

I take it from him. I see he is also holding my phone in his hands. He types something in before handing it to me as well.

"I put my number in your phone."

"What makes you think I want that?"

He cocks his head to the side as he stares at me. "You will. I have a feeling you will want it really soon."

God, this man is arrogant, but his confidence is alluring. I could use an ounce or two of his confidence, if only for a day. Maybe then I wouldn't be marrying a complete stranger in six months.

I walk to the door. He follows.

I open the door and stand in the doorway. "Thanks for the wine and—"

His lips crash with mine before I can say anything. He's promising more, I realize. With his tongue pushing further into my mouth, he's demanding I call him.

When we finally break away, my breathing is fast, much too fast. I touch my hands to my chest, trying to calm my breathing. I stare at him for a second longer before turning to leave without a word.

"Don't run anymore. You're stronger than you think."

I pause at his words, but I don't turn around. He doesn't follow me or say anything else.

He's left me his number to call. And I will. I'll call. He knows it as well as I do.

I walk into the elevator alone. I touch my fingers to my lips still tingling from his kiss, a kiss I want more of. Maybe he's the answer. He's smart, probably a businessman. He's older and responsible. There's not a tattoo or piercing on his body—at least not one I noticed.

What if I found someone capable of running the company on my own? What if I found my own love? Then, I could marry who I wanted while still making sure the company would be in good hands.

I have to find a way to convince Granddad. I need to find a way to buy myself some time. And introducing Granddad to Killian might be the way. I could show him I am capable of dating strong, intelligent men.

Killian might not be the best choice, but right now, he's my only choice. Maybe he's the right choice.

5

I step foot back inside the Felton Grand. Even though I was just in the hotel earlier when I was with Killian, this is the first time since my father's death I've really let myself take in the casino. Last night I let Killian rush me to his room as fast as possible. Now, I'm walking slowly, taking in everything.

I notice the gentle calming sound of the expansive fountain at the entrance to the hotel. I see the light twinkling off the water from the large crystal chandelier overhead.

I walk through the long hallways filled with shops and restaurants. The hallways are calm. It's early, and only a few people have woken up to enjoy breakfast at one of the many restaurants. I smile as I look up and see the details of the arched ceiling overhead. When I was a kid, I used to lie on a bench in the hallway and stare up at this beautiful ceiling.

I walk to the casino floor. I take a deep breath. I feel my father all around as I walk past the flashing lights of the slot machines. This is where my father spent most of his time— here on the floor of the casino, mingling with guests and making sure everything was running smoothly.

I walk off the casino floor to a door that says *Employees Only*. I flash my card on a sensor and watch as the light changes from red to green before I open the door. I enter and take the stairs up to the second floor.

I take a right and head down to my father's office at the end of the long hallway. I take the key out of my pocket and unlock the door. I push it open, and the smell immediately overwhelms me. It smells like expensive cologne and cigars. It smells like my father.

I miss you, I think as I walk in and close the door behind me.

Tears fall fast as I make my way over to my favorite couch on one side of my father's office. I let them. I cry. I let everything out. I let go of the pain. I let go of the guilt. I let go of all of it. It all comes out.

When the final bits of pain and guilt have washed away, all I'm left with is anxiety over speaking to Granddad. I begin pacing back and forth in my father's large office while I wait for my grandfather to arrive.

I can do this. I can do this. I can do this.

I try to keep my eyes on the ground instead of looking at the numerous reminders of my father.

I don't have to look up to know a picture of Dad and me is sitting on his desk. I was five, riding on his shoulders. There's another of the whole family sitting beside it.

I don't have to look up to know the most comfortable couch on the planet is leaning against the far wall. I have fallen asleep on it countless times while reading a book, waiting for Dad to take me out to dinner.

I don't have to look up to know a considerable stack of every magazine I modeled in is piled in the corner.

I don't have to look up to know a picture of my first modeling job when I was twelve is in a frame on the wall.

Instead, I try to rehearse what I'm going to say when my grandfather gets here. *Granddad, I love you and respect you, but I'm an adult. I can make my own decisions in the best interests of myself and this company. I've already found someone who I think would make a good candidate, and with time I know I can find the perfect man...*

I keep repeating the speech I practiced all night, but my mind quickly goes back to Killian. I bite my lip, remembering how his lips felt on mine, how he pulled every emotion out of me. I tuck my hair behind my ear, recalling how his touch against my neck sent shivers all over my body. My heart speeds up as I think about how I had the most explosive orgasm of my life with his tongue buried inside me.

I try to stop thinking about Killian, but I can't. I haven't called him yet. It's only been a few hours since I saw him, but I have a feeling I'll be looking for something comforting after this meeting, and I will need someone to talk to. No, I'll need someone to help me forget. I'll text him this afternoon. It won't hurt to ask if he is free.

"You're on time," Granddad says as he walks into the office.

"Yes," I say as I stop pacing. I immediately forget about Killian. I know my face is flushed, so without having to look up, I walk to the corner of the room where there is a container of water. I take one of the white plastic cups and fill it with water before walking slowly to a chair in front of the desk.

I slowly sip my water, trying to drain my face of its overly pink color, while stalling from giving my speech. *I'll wait just a few minutes longer—no need to rush the speech and get it wrong.*

"He should be here soon," Granddad says, staring at his watch, as he sits behind the desk my father used to.

I don't think I could ever sit there. That's Dad's chair, not his.

"Last time I spoke with him, he was just wrapping up a meeting."

I nod and drink my water faster. I don't have much time then.

"Granddad, I've been thinking. I, uh...?" I start talking, but I have no idea what I'm saying. "I, um...I don't think marrying whoever is going to walk through that door is the best idea. I think...I think I should have a say in who I marry." I make the mistake of looking up to see Granddad frowning at me with his eyes raised, but it doesn't stop my mouth from spilling every dumb thought on my brain. "I think I've already found someone whom I could fall for. He's smart and handsome, and I think you will like him. He's a businessman. And he's a great kisser." *Damn it, why did I say that?*

"Hush, girl," he says.

But I don't hush. I keep talking. "And I don't think I even want to get married anytime soon. I want to find more men to kiss. I'm young, much too young to get married this year. I need to live a little first. And if I'm honest, I think I could run the company by myself without a husband by my side. I think that's what Dad would have wanted."

"Hush," he says more sternly this time.

I stop, mainly because I can't believe the words that just came out of my mouth. *What the hell has come over me? I don't want to run the company myself, do I?*

I grab my cup of water sitting on the edge of the desk with shaky hands. I take a long sip, waiting for the lecture.

But it never comes.

I hear a deep voice clear his throat from behind me. I don't have to look up to know the man I'm supposed to marry is standing in the doorway. I just hope he wasn't standing there long enough to hear that embarrassing speech.

"Come on in, son," Granddad says, standing from the desk with a massive smile on his face.

I'm screwed. He just called this man son. He's probably more in love with this guy than he is with me. And after my epic speech, I have no doubt I'll be marrying the man behind me.

"I would like to introduce you to my granddaughter, Kinsley," he says, as he walks toward the man behind me.

I take one last sip of water before I plaster on the biggest fake smile I can manage while I turn to meet my future husband. I wonder if he knows. *Has he already been told to get complete control of the company, he is going to have to marry me? Or is he blissfully ignorant to that fact?*

I bring my eyes up to face my future husband. The man standing in front of me isn't my future husband. He isn't a complete stranger. It's Killian.

I choke. That's what stupid thing I do in response to seeing the man who had his tongue down my throat only hours earlier. I cough and choke on the remnants of the water still clinging to my throat. That's what I do while I watch my grandfather place his hand on the shoulder of the man who just gave me my first orgasm that wasn't given by a vibrator.

"Are you okay?" Killian asks.

I nod as I choke again. I grab my throat, trying to get it to stop. It doesn't, not until I get three more coughs in, causing my cheeks to turn an even brighter shade of pink.

When I finally lift my eyes back up, I see two pairs of

eyes intently staring at me. One pair looks at me with concern, the other looks at me with shame.

I try to recompose myself by bringing back the smile I wore moments earlier.

"Let's try that again," Granddad says. "I would like to introduce you to my beautiful granddaughter, Kinsley Felton."

"Kinsley, this is Killian Browne."

Killian steps forward and extends his hand to me. I slowly place mine in his, already anticipating how his firm handshake is going to start tiny fireworks inside me. It does the second his hand touches mine.

"Pleasure to meet you, Ms. Felton."

I narrow my eyes but nod anyway. He's not going to let on we have already met. I'm grateful.

I notice Granddad smiling brightly behind him at our encounter.

"Please take a seat. We have lots to talk about," Granddad says as he retakes the seat behind the desk.

I walk back to my chair, aware of Killian's eyes taking in all of me from my high heels to my knee-length high-waist pencil skirt to my magenta top.

I sit down and glance at him sitting in the chair next to me.

Killian looks much the same as he did last night. He's in a nicely fitted suit with a blue tie. His hair is gelled slightly to keep it spiked to the side. The only difference is his five o'clock shadow is gone.

I look back to myself. I look entirely different from the last time he saw me. I'm no longer wearing casual attire. Makeup covers every flaw I showed him before. My long, hair is perfectly curled into flowing locks free of the frizz from our night together.

Does Killian know why he's here—to marry me? Is that what he was referencing this morning when he talked about family obligations? Is he being forced to marry by his family? Did he know when he saw me at that table last night I was whom he was going to marry?

No, there's no way. He would have said something. He wouldn't have led me on like that.

"You both know why you're here, so let's get started on some of the details."

I nod and see Killian nodding stoically next to me. *So, he does know he's here to marry me?*

"My son and I thought you two would make a perfect match. Kinsley is about to graduate from Yale. She's an experienced model. She's beautiful."

Killian nods, but he doesn't say anything as Granddad tries to sell me to him.

Granddad turns to face me now. "Killian has been working for the company for five years. He graduated from Harvard. He is our current VP of Casino Operations. He's intelligent, ambitious, confident, focused, decisive, and professional."

I nod at my grandfather, disappointed he's listed several positive personality traits of Killian's, while I only got beautiful. That's all I am to these men.

I watch as he digs in the desk drawer before pulling out a stack of papers. He hands one stack to me and one to Killian.

"These are the terms of Robert's will. It includes everything the two of you need to do to inherit his shares of the company. There is also a copy of my will and what you will need to do to get my shares as well. It includes what we expect before we'll make you CEO, Killian," he says, staring at Killian now.

Killian nods.

"Both of you need to read it over in the next couple of days, so you understand everything." He focuses his attention on Killian, like he is the only one who gets a say in any of this. "You have one month to decide. That's all I can give you. I'll need an answer then."

"Of course," Killian says. He glances down at his watch. "I'm sorry to cut this meeting short, but I have another meeting I need to get to."

Granddad stands, smiling. "Don't worry, Killian. I'm having Tony cover the meeting today. Instead, I have a reservation for you two at a restaurant downstairs."

"Sir, I'm not sure Tony is the best man for the job. He's not up-to-date yet on the new systems."

"I agree, but this"—Granddad points to me and then back to Killian—"is a more pressing issue at the moment."

Killian glares at my grandfather but doesn't argue again.

He turns to me. "Would you like to have lunch with me?"

"Yes." My answer isn't forced. I want to have lunch with Killian.

I have a lot of questions for him. *Why the hell did he agree to marry a complete stranger? Did he know who I was when he stared at me from across the blackjack table? Did he know when he got me into his bed and fucked me with his tongue? I'm afraid Killian's answer to all those questions will be a resounding yes.*

6

I STARE DOWN at the menu. I haven't said a word since we left my father's office. Killian hasn't either. I think he's giving me time to process everything. I try to look at the menu to at least make up my mind on what I'm going to eat. Then, I can focus on what just happened.

"What can I get you?" the bubbly waitress asks.

"Um..." I say. I take a deep breath, trying to decide what wine I want. I want wine—no, I *need* wine to get through this, but I have no idea about wines. I eye a delicious-looking cheeseburger as a waitress passes by with it before placing it on the table next to us. A cheeseburger sounds good. Or maybe I should eat something a little lighter and healthier. Or maybe I'll have the pizza. That's what my father and I would always share when we came here.

"We will both have a glass of Chateau Margaux Bordeaux '61, if you have it. If not, then '82. We will have the vegetables and hummus appetizer. And we will both have the salmon with asparagus."

I glare at Killian as the waitress takes our menus away.

"What was that?"

"What?" he asks innocently.

"Why did you order for me? And why did you order the salmon? I'm not a health nut like you. I wanted the burger." *Yes, definitely the burger. Or the pizza.*

"Health nut, huh?" He casually leans back in his chair. "I didn't want to give you too much to think about right now. I knew you liked the wine, and after the breakfast you had, you need some vegetables and healthy protein to keep you going today."

I shake my head. "You have no idea what I need."

The waitress quickly brings the wine, and I'm at least thankful he ordered my favorite wine.

"I'll have the cheeseburger and fries, actually." The waitress gives me a disapproving nod before leaving.

I sigh as I sip my wine and try to process what just happened, so I'll know where to start with my questioning. My brain immediately goes to the moment in my father's office. I literally choked. *God, that was so embarrassing.*

What was surprising was *Killian's* reaction. When he saw me, he didn't seem the least bit surprised. Not even the best actor in the world would have been able to hide some sort of reaction of surprise when he saw me. I've studied enough actors' reactions to know a truthful one from a fake one. His was truthful.

I deepen my glare. "You already knew who I was. Last night, when you saw me at that blackjack table, you already knew who I was."

"Yes," he says.

"Why would you do that? Why would you lead me on like that when you already knew? You lied to me! You made me believe I could find someone on my own. Instead, you were prearranged. Did my grandfather put you up to it? Did he want you to seduce me before we met? Did you two think I would be happy then, if I already liked you when I found out it was you?"

My face flushes bright red again, but this time, it's mostly out of anger and only a little bit from embarrassment. Everyone knew, except for me.

"I didn't initially go to the casino seeking you out last night. I went there for the same reason as you, I'm guessing. I was mourning a man I deeply cared about, and I thought gambling like I used to with him would be the best way to honor that man."

"Wait, my father went gambling with you?"

"Yes. I worked very closely with your father over the last five years. He was a great mentor to me. When we flew to different cities for meetings, we would gamble at various casinos. It was the best way to learn from the competition. Robert was a great man. I miss him."

"Don't," I say, my voice trembling. "Don't. You don't get to miss him. You don't get to mourn him like I do. He's not your father."

The guilt immediately comes back. This man spent time with my father when I didn't. I should have been there for him when he died. I should have gone to college closer to home so I could have spent more time with him. Instead, I was happy to get as far away as possible when my family suggested Yale.

"Oh, princess, I could never miss him like you do, but I still miss him."

I freeze when he says the nickname he has adapted for me...except he didn't come up with my name. My father did.

"You got it from him."

His eyes narrow in response, but he has no clue what I'm talking about.

"You got the princess nickname from my father. That's all he ever called me. I'm sure if you hung out so much together, you heard him talk about me in that manner. Don't call me princess—ever again."

He looks sad when I say that, but I can't deal with this. I can't deal with the fact that he got to spend so much time with my father in his final years while I was away at school and got so little time. My life isn't fair.

I feel the tears welling in my eyes, but I don't let them out. Killian doesn't deserve any of my tears. He doesn't deserve to see me mourn a man who was mine, not his.

The waitress places our appetizer in front of us. It looks disgusting. A mush of stuff sits in the middle with raw carrots, cucumbers, and celeries lining the outside. I don't touch it. Instead, I lift the wine glass back to my lips.

I have so many questions. I don't even know where to start. So, I sit and watch as Killian fills a plate with hummus and vegetables. Then, to my surprise, he places the plate in front of me before filling another one.

"Eat," he says.

My stomach grumbles, so I do, but it's not because he tells me to. I try the carrot in the mush. It's not half bad, I realize, as I crunch on the vegetable, but I'm not going to let him know that.

"Ask me," he says before taking a bite of his food.

"What?"

"Ask me everything."

"When did you find out?" I ask hesitantly.

"When did I find out that your father wanted me to marry you before he would make me CEO?"

I nod, unable to say any words.

"Three years ago. It was when he promoted me to VP."

My eyes are wide. He's known for three years that he's

going to marry me. He could have come up to me at any point in those three years and told me. He could have at least introduced himself to me. He could have done anything, but he didn't.

"Why didn't you tell me?"

He runs his hand through his hair, slightly messing it up, but somehow, it looks even better. "I wanted to. I learned a lot about you from your father. I stalked you on social media. I quickly realized your father was right. You weren't ready to meet me. You were too young and naive to meet whom you were supposed to marry. You're still too young."

"I am not!" I protest.

He smiles a smug smile. "Yes, you are."

"Then, why did you agree to marry me if I'm so young and naive?"

"I haven't yet."

My eyes grow wide at his response.

"What do you mean, you haven't yet? I thought..."

"I told your father I would think about it, but I've never really had any intention of marrying anybody—ever. I'm perfectly content as I am."

"Then, why are you here? If you are not going to marry me, why are you here?"

He looks smugly past me as he contemplates his answer. "Because I want to be CEO. I've earned it. And I'll marry you, if I have to, to get it, but I think there is another way, a better way."

His words sting. It stings a lot to hear him say he doesn't want to marry me even though I don't want to marry him either.

"What was last night then? Why did you almost sleep with me if you didn't want to marry me?"

He cocks his head and smirks at me. "I can fuck a

woman without marrying her. And, if I recall, we never got around to the fucking."

I wince every time he says the word *fuck*. I'm not used to men using language like that around me. Although it usually sounds sexy when falling from his lips, right now, it feels like a punch to the gut.

"Why were you at the casino last night?" I barely whisper.

"As I said earlier, I didn't go into that casino seeking you out. I saw you at that table, and I thought it would be fun to mess with you. After watching you for a while, I found you were almost a complete contradiction from everything I had known about you. You seemed confident at that table, sure of yourself. You didn't seem like the naive young girl I'd thought you were."

"And now?"

He sighs. "I still think you are a naive young princess."

I glare at him when he says the last word. "You're wrong."

The waitress interrupts us, bringing us plates of salmon with asparagus and my cheeseburger. I dig in. Otherwise, I might do something stupid, like climb over the table and ring Killian's neck.

"I know you went to Yale to study theater. Who does that? You don't go to Yale to study theater. You go to Yale to study business or economics or finance—something useful."

He pauses to take a bite while I continue shoving my own food in my mouth, trying my best to remain calm and poised, like I've been taught to do.

"I know you modeled for *Seventeen* magazine along with a slew of other teenage magazines. You're beautiful; it comes easily to you."

I take another bite. I feel the tears welling again, but I hold them back. *Do not cry.*

"I know you haven't been on a date in three years. That's why you needed a release last night. I know you have never made one goddamn decision by yourself. You want to know how I know that? You texted your father every five fucking minutes, asking him for advice."

A tear falls, just one single tear. I hate him. I loved my father and would do anything for him. Even marrying this asshole in front of me if my father thought it was for the best. And Killian is using my love for my father to hurt me.

"I know because you are the reason this has gotten this far. If you had stood up to your father before he died, you wouldn't be getting forced into a marriage you didn't want. And don't tell me you want this. I know what you were running from last night. It's *this*. You were running away from being forced into an arranged marriage."

I wipe the tear from my eye. "Stop!" I say a little too loudly. I notice the stares from the table closest to us, and I try to adjust my voice to not bring any more attention to us.

"Well, you were running, too. I don't have to have studied everything about you for three years to know everything I need to know about you. You're an arrogant, bossy ass. Everything in your life revolves around work. You don't date because you don't have time. You find any attractive woman you can at bars to pick up and take home for one night. And, worst of all, you must not be that good at your job if the only way you can get the CEO position you are so desperate for, is to marry the previous CEO's daughter. The only reason they chose you and not someone more qualified is because you are the only man in an executive position who's anywhere near my age," I say, having no idea where those words came from. I've never been this outspoken in my entire life.

I stare at my now empty plate I didn't even realize I had been eating.

"Feel better now?" he asks calmly.

He stares at me, completely unaffected by my words, which makes me even angrier.

"Yes," I spout.

He eyes my empty plate as my stomach rumbles again. "You should have stuck with the salmon, and then you wouldn't still feel hungry."

"I'm not hungry," I say, acting like a defiant child as my stomach growls again feeling bloated and hungry. *God, no wonder he thinks I'm like a child. I act like one.*

His bottom lip twitches in a smile.

"So, what do we do now? What's your fabulous plan?"

"My plan is for Lee to realize how valuable I am to the company—so valuable he will want me to be CEO whether or not I marry his granddaughter. I already had Robert convinced. I can convince your grandfather, too."

"That's not going to work. They want the company to stay in the family."

"That's where you come in. You need to tell him that you are so devastated by your father's death you don't want anything to do with the company. You don't want it. You'll marry someone else who your grandfather wants when you are older but not now. And, no matter what, you want nothing to do with the Felton Corporation. All you want is what you already have—plenty of money to live by."

I stand up and throw my napkin on the table before I storm off. I'm so tired of listening to what other people tell me I should be doing. Killian doesn't say a word, and he doesn't stop me from leaving the table.

I wander down the hallways of the largest casino and hotel in the Felton empire. It's the original one, the one that started it all. This one isn't my favorite though. My favorite, Crystal Waterfalls, is farther down on the strip. It has a river and a waterfall flowing through it. But Felton Grand has its charms, too. It's flashy and brings the hustle and bustle of the city inside.

It could work. I know it could. I'm already devastated. I could convince Granddad I'd lose my mind if I had to step foot inside one of the casinos again. *But is that what I want? Is that what my father would have wanted for me? Did he really tell Killian he wanted him to run the company without marrying me? Don't I want at least some small part of the company for myself?*

I try to think about what I want, but all I come up with is what I don't want. I don't want to marry Killian. At least, I don't want to be forced into marrying him, especially now I know he doesn't want to marry me either.

I don't know what *I* want. So, instead, I try to think about what my father would have wanted. *Did he ever give any indication he didn't want me to marry Killian? Did he ever give me any clue of what he did want me to do?*

One memory pushes into my head. The memory used to seem so unimportant, but maybe it means more than I know.

"What does my princess want to be when she grows up?"

I think for a minute as I put another block on top of the one my father placed. "A princess!" I shout.

He laughs. "Of course! You already are a princess. And when you're old enough, I'll make sure you have a castle and a whole empire to run, if you want it. But what else do you want to be?"

My five-year-old self thinks harder this time. What else do I want to be, other than a princess? "I know! I want to be a CEOOOO, like you, Daddy!"

He smiles and thinks seriously for a second. "If that's what you want someday, it's yours. You can be anything you want, no matter what Granddad or I tell you."

"Yay! I'm going to be a CEEEAAA, like you!" I squeal.

"Shh," he says. "You have to keep it a secret though."

I pretend to lock my mouth with a fake key, like I do whenever anybody else tells me a secret. My father laughs again. He's always laughing at me, and I love to make him laugh.

"For now though, let's just say you want to be a princess."

"Princess Kinsley and King Daddy!"

I've never thought about that memory—until now. I don't even know if my father was serious when he said I could be CEO. And I never thought to ask. I never thought I wanted to run a company. I don't have the talent, the skills, or schooling. But maybe it's what I want—to follow in my father's footsteps. It's all I've ever wanted—to be just like him.

I make my way back to the table and find my plate has been taken away. In its place is a piece of chocolate cake and ice cream. Confused, I look up at Killian.

He shrugs. "To make up for not letting you order your own food and for telling you what to do. I was wrong. I'm sorry. Don't all girls love chocolate?"

I smile. Killian does have some good qualities to him when he's not being a bossy, arrogant ass. I dig in and melt in my seat as the ice cream melts in my mouth. I forget about everything, except for how good this tastes in my mouth.

"So, you'll agree to the plan then?" Killian asks, seeming slightly nervous for the first time since I've met him.

I take one more bite. Chewing slowly, I savor every last drop in my mouth.

"Maybe," I say on autopilot.

He smiles, thinking he's won.

"I mean...no," I say, realizing my screw-up. "I don't think your plan will work."

"Then, what do you propose?"

I wince at the word *propose*. That's what will happen if I don't find a way out of this. If my plan fails, it will end with Killian proposing to me. It's not that I wouldn't want to look at a handsome man like Killian for all of eternity, but he doesn't want me in return.

"I propose you find a new company that will make you CEO because the current position is already taken."

"By whom?"

"Me."

He laughs, hard and uncontrollably. And then he laughs some more while I sit in my seat, frowning. When he finally stops, he seriously looks at me. "You can't be serious?"

"I am."

"You can't make a decision to save your life. You can't even choose what you want to eat in a timely manner. You have no skill set. You don't have a college degree. The only thing you have going for you is..."

"My beauty."

"No." His eyes meet mine. "I was going to say that you're family."

I shake my head. He's wrong about that one. Granddad doesn't care I'm part of the family. He already thinks I will make a terrible candidate for CEO even though the company has been passed down to members of the family for three generations now. He's only willing to pass it down to my husband. My beauty is the only thing I have going for me.

"Well, this should get interesting. But go ahead and try. This week is going to be amusing."

"I will." I stand from the table while digging into my purse to throw some cash on the table.

He grabs my arm again, keeping me from walking out. He pulls me close to him so he can speak into my ear, but this time, there is nothing sexy about the move. "And when you realize what a mistake you've made, call me, and then I can work out a real plan to save you from marrying an arrogant, bossy ass like me," he says, repeating the names I called him earlier. "Because trust me, princess, nobody wants that."

"I don't have..." That's when I remember I already have his phone number.

"Although you should probably change the name in your phone to arrogant, bossy ass. I kind of like that." He winks at me.

I pull away from his grasp and run out of the restaurant. He's right. I don't want to marry him, not now after the conversation we just had. I wouldn't marry him if he were my only choice.

I don't know what to choose. One, marry Killian and be everything my family has always wanted. Two, refuse and be shamed by my family forever. Or, three, convince my grandfather I can run the company—just like my father, just like my grandfather, and just like my great-grandfather. I'm not sure. The only option I'm convinced I don't want is number one. I don't want to marry Killian.

7

———

"REALLY?" I ask into the phone.

"Yes. Your grades were high enough you could graduate without making up your final exams. Of course, if you would like to make them up, your last semester grades would improve."

"No. The grades can stay as they are." I release a sigh of relief.

"Okay then. We will mail you your degree. Congratulations, Ms. Felton."

I end the call as I hear the door open to my childhood bedroom. I turn and smile at Scarlett.

"Hey, bitch," Scarlett says as she makes herself at home on my bed.

"Hey," I say, shaking my head at her words. "Are you all moved in?"

Scarlett sighs. "No. The movers are impossible. They have been at my new house all day, and they've only moved in half of my stuff. They said it would take them another day to finish. So, I'm stuck at my parents' house for another night."

"I don't know how you'll survive," I say sarcastically.

"You really have no idea how bad it is. All I hear about is how I don't have any jobs lined up. I don't have a serious boyfriend. What am I going to do with my life?" She sighs again. "It's exhausting. I don't know how you can stand to stay here with your mother and grandfather. Why don't you find a house or at least an apartment to move into?"

I glance at Scarlett, who is now flipping through the papers Granddad gave me. I walk over and snatch them out of her hands.

"Those were boring anyway."

I shake my head. "I'll move out soon. I just haven't put much thought into where I want to live."

"So, how did it go, meeting the future Mr. Felton?"

I put the papers back on my desk. I spent all night reading every detail of my father's and my granddad's wills. I'm screwed. If I want any equity, any money, the only way is to marry Killian.

I bite my lip as I turn to face her. "Not well."

Scarlett sits up in my bed. "Why? Is he ugly? Or, no...is he, like, fifty years old or something? Does he have a disgusting mole on his face? Is he bald? Doesn't speak English? Fat? What?"

I pace my room, occasionally stopping to stare at Scarlett. "No."

"What is it?"

"Remember that guy I told you about? The one I met at the casino the other night?"

Scarlett crawls forward on my bed until she is lying on her stomach. "You mean, the mysterious, sexy man who gave you the only orgasm of your life?"

"Best, not only." I pace. "And, yes. It was him."

She scrunches her nose at me. "What?"

"The man I'm supposed to marry is Killian, the same man who gave me the orgasm the other night."

A sly smile spreads across her lips. "So, what's the problem?"

"He doesn't want to marry me."

"That's crazy. Everybody wants to marry you. Why doesn't he want to marry you?"

I grab my forehead that is pounding from her insane questioning.

"I say, fuck him!" she says after a few minutes.

"What?"

"Have sex with him. Once he gets a taste of Kinsley Felton, he will want more and more. He'll be begging you to marry him."

I chuckle. "I don't think that is going to happen. He thinks of me as a child."

"Ew. He does not, or he wouldn't have done what he did to you the other night."

"He was just messing with me."

"No, Kins, he wasn't. He was into you."

"Whatever, I don't want to marry him anyway."

"What? I thought you said he was sexy. I thought..."

"I don't want to marry him because maybe I want to be CEO. I don't want to have to marry someone else in order to have anything to do with the company. Or maybe I don't want anything to do with the company."

Silence. That's the answer I get.

"Scar?"

"Yeah?" she says hesitantly.

"Well?"

"I don't know, Kins. Running the company is a lot of responsibility. Are you sure you are up for that?"

"I don't know."

She laughs. "See? You can't even honestly answer a simple question. How do you expect to run a huge company where you are going to have to answer, like, a million questions a minute?" She pauses. "I don't know, Kins. But if I were you, I'd fuck the guy. That's what I would do. It's a lot more fun."

"Thanks, Scar. You're a real help," I say sarcastically.

"Kinsley!" my mother screams from downstairs.

"That's my cue to leave," Scarlett says.

I nod. "I'll tell you how it goes later."

Scarlett quickly hugs me. "I know you are still sad about your dad. And I know you don't want to deal with everything right now, but I'm always here for you if you need me."

I nod, and then she slips out of my room.

I grab my purse, so I can get out of here as soon as I deal with my mother. I take the stairs down two at a time and find my mother in the kitchen.

She's slumped over the bar. She's not crying, but she doesn't exactly look her best in my father's old robe. Her hair is matted on her head. She's a mess, but at least she left her room.

"Morning, Mom," I say as I open the pantry to find a granola bar.

"Where's the alcohol?"

I take a deep breath before answering, "What do you mean?"

"The alcohol we always keep in the bar. Where is it?"

I shrug. "I don't know, Mom. I think everybody drank it all after the funeral." That's not true. I know exactly where the alcohol is because I'm the one who took it.

It's been years since my mother relapsed. She's been

sober for almost five years now. She cleaned up when I almost destroyed our family.

Dad dying must have pushed her back to the alcohol. I don't blame her. We all miss Dad. And we all deal with losing him in different ways. I just can't handle the way she has chosen to deal with his death.

I glance at my phone. Her old therapist and AA sponsor should be here soon to help her since I can't. I know from experience. I don't have the patience to help her.

"I need the alcohol, damn it!"

I calmly walk over to my mother. "I'll make sure to have someone pick you up some alcohol on their way in today. But, right now, I think you need to eat. Can I make you something?"

She grabs the closest vase of flowers and slams it to the floor. I jump at the sound of the glass breaking on the floor. I don't react to her tantrum. Even though I've wanted to do the same thing to the stupid vases of flowers, I can't show her it's okay.

"Hi, Mrs. Felton. Let me make you some breakfast," Samantha, one of our cooks, says as she enters the kitchen, seeing the mess.

I go over and clean up the glass while Samantha has my mother's attention.

When I'm finished, I whisper to Samantha, "Just keep an eye on her until Dennis and Kirsten get her. Half hour, max."

She nods and smiles before going back to cooking my mother some pancakes. I walk out of the kitchen to the front door. I need to move out of here. I don't know how much more of this I can handle.

"Where are you going?" Granddad asks as I try to leave.

"To the Felton Grand."

He curiously looks at me even though it's not that strange for me to go to the casino. I used to go all the time before I went off to college. It should be understandable I would want to mourn my father there.

"I'm sorry," he says as he looks at me. For the first time since the funeral, I see tears in his eyes. "I'm sorry for blaming you. It's not your fault. I need you to know that."

I walk over and hug him. I know he needs me to forgive him for blaming me just as much as I need to stop blaming myself for my father's death. But I'm not sure I can do either of those things yet. I'm not ready to forgive.

"I miss him," is what I say instead.

"Me, too, sweetie. Me, too." He gently rubs my back, like a grandfather should. "Do you want some company?"

"No, I just want to spend some time by myself," I lie.

I try not to look him in the eyes, so he won't know I'm lying, but somehow, he does. Everyone can always tell when I'm lying. It's one of the reasons I would make a terrible actress.

I don't want him to come with me though. I need some time to interact with everyone at the casino, to begin to form real relationships with them, to begin to understand how the business runs. That way, when I tell him I want to run the company, I will have some ammunition to do it with.

Then, Granddad smiles, like he just realized something. I stare at him with a blank expression.

"Ah, you're going to see Killian. That's why you don't want me to come with you."

I blush at his words, bringing more truth to them in his eyes.

He smiles wider. "Have you fallen for that boy already?"

"No, Granddad. I just need some time to myself."

He nods knowingly. "Just let me know when he's wrapped around your finger so I can set the date."

"Granddad!"

He winks at me before heading into the kitchen to be with my mother. I sigh. But, at least, if he thinks I'm into Killian, he won't think anything of me spending time at the casino in the upcoming days, which will come in handy since I plan on spending lots of time there. It'll be enough time to make up my mind.

The only problem is, I haven't been able to get Killian out of my head. Anytime I'm not missing my dad; I'm lusting after Killian. I miss the taste of his lips. I miss his hands on my body. I miss his tongue on my clit. I miss screaming his name when I come. Most of all, I miss that I never got to feel him inside me. And, now, I'm never going to.

8

———

I'VE SPENT the last three hours sitting behind my father's desk, reading anything I can find that will catch me up on the direction of the company. The only problem is, I haven't learned much. Most of the files that would be of any importance are locked away in the file cabinet or on his computer, which is also locked.

There are a couple of reports showing decreasing sales in two casinos, but when I look at the numbers, it's easy to see the most important figures haven't been plotted. With just a few changes, the reports would show the casinos had been increasing in sales from month to month. At least, that's what makes sense to me, but maybe I'm missing something.

I sigh when I look through the last piece of paper that has anything to do with the company. I just wasted three hours and am no better off for it. I'm not sure I'm going to be able to do this, not unless I find the key to my father's filing cabinets or his password for his computer.

Granddad would know, but I can't ask him. I guess I'll just have to learn about the company elsewhere. I don't know how though. That's probably why I've been hiding out in my father's office for the last few hours.

I get up from the desk and poke my head into the hallway. It seems relatively empty for a Thursday. I'm surprised no one has come into my father's office all morning. It's probably because everyone is too sad to think of him as gone. I know everyone loved him. He was a great boss, a great friend, a great husband, and a great father. At least, that's what the minister said at his funeral. I choose to believe that.

I step into the hallway and start walking. I don't know where I'm going. I just go.

"Hi, Ms. Felton."

"Tony," I say before hugging the man who is practically a member of the family. He always seemed like a brother to my father.

"How are you doing?" he asks the token question.

"I'm holding up."

"You visiting your father's office?" He nods in the direction of the office.

I nod.

"I haven't built up the courage to go in there yet. When I do, I know I'll end up crying like a weepy old man."

I smile. "We can't have that."

"I should get back to work. I hope to see more of you around, Ms. Felton."

I smile and start walking again. "Wait," I say, turning around. "Do you mind if I hang out with you today? I want to be around people who knew my father. It feels like home here, not like at the house."

Tony looks at me with confusion. "Are you sure? It's going to be pretty boring. I have some phone conferences, and then I really need to get the numbers ready for the expansion Mr. Browne asked for."

I smile. Tony has already given me more information about the company than I found all morning.

"Yes, I'm sure." I take his arm and walk with him to his office. "And call me Kinsley, Tony. We are practically family."

———

Oh my God! This office is a mess. It looks like a tornado came in here and blew papers into disastrous piles all around the room.

Tony, on the other hand, walks into his office with no surprise on his face. He doesn't react like someone just came in here and ransacked his office. He actually seems to relax when he enters his office.

I walk over to his desk as Tony takes a seat behind it.

"I have to take a quick phone call, but make yourself at home. Then, I can show you some of the stuff your father and I were working on," he says.

I nod and do my best to smile as I glance around the smaller-size office, but I'm afraid it comes across as a frown or a horribly disgusted grimace. I cover my mouth with my hand, hoping he didn't see. He brightly smiles back at me. I guess he didn't.

He begins dialing his phone. I wait until I hear him chattering away at someone, paying me no attention, before I take a seat on the floor in front of piles of paper.

I feel bad for Tony. He's my father's age. He's worked for the company almost as long as my father, but he will never become CEO, never even be given a chance. Instead, he will always be just the Assistant to the VP of Operations. He's

Killian's assistant, I realize, even though Killian has only worked for the company for five years, and Tony has worked for the company for thirty. To a company this big, it doesn't matter who is more loyal. It matters who is more likely to get results. And after I look around this office, I know why Tony will never reach a higher position. His office is a mess. There is no way he can be organized in a mess like this.

I still feel sorry for him though. Even though I know Tony gets paid generously to do this job, I still feel sad. I have a better chance of becoming CEO than Tony ever will.

And if I am CEO, I will have to make tough decisions, like promoting a less experienced, younger employee over a loyal and mature employee. That is probably an easy decision compared with the choices my dad made on a daily basis. I'm not sure I can do it.

I swallow hard and push the thoughts out of my head. I'm not here to think about if I can make the tough decisions required of the job right now. I'm here to learn as much as I can about the company and the job. Then, I can make decisions about my future.

I dig into the pile, trying to figure out what I'm looking at. There are hundreds and hundreds of more charts and graphs with the same incorrect information on them as the ones in my father's office. *Shit.* I hope my dad wasn't relying on them to make decisions about the company. I hope Killian isn't either.

I look at the name on them, trying to figure out who made the graphs and who wrote the reports, so I can tell Killian he needs to fire them. Then, I see it. It's Tony. He created these graphs. If anybody ever found out, he'd be fired. My dad was the only one who would care if Tony still worked for the company or not.

I sigh. Now, not only do I have to learn about the company, but I also have to find a way to make sure Tony gets better at making graphs, so he isn't out of a job.

I give up sorting the mess of papers when I hear Tony end the call. I stand and walk over to his desk with a smile on my face. He looks stressed as he shuffles papers around on his desk before switching on his computer.

"Mr. Browne and Mr. Felton wanted to expand this hotel and casino to allow for more high-roller rooms."

I nod as I walk over to stand behind him. "Makes sense. So, what's the problem?"

Tony sighs as his elbow knocks some papers off his desk. He watches them scatter onto the floor of his office, but he doesn't bother to pick them up. He turns to his computer instead. "The numbers don't support doing an expansion."

"Do you mind if I take a look at them?" I bat my eyes and smile as sweetly as possible at him.

"Be my guest," he says, getting up from his chair.

I take his seat, but I don't want him here when I change everything. I don't want him to know how badly he screwed up. I need to find a way to teach him. But that isn't right now. Right now, I need to fix this before he passes it along to Killian or anyone else who might fire him.

"Tony, do you mind getting me a coffee?" I ask. I yawn, bringing more credibility to my lie. *It isn't really a lie*, I reason with myself. I could use a coffee. I didn't sleep much last night, and I woke up earlier than I'm used to in order to have a full day here.

He smiles and nods. "I'll be right back."

As soon as he leaves, I turn my attention back to the screen. Everything is a mess. Everything is wrong. I pull up a new spreadsheet to start over because it's not worth fixing what he's already done.

I let my fingers fly over the keys as I type in every figure that I can find into the new data points. I love the rush I get as I enter in all the data. I love how it feels to use my brain for something other than deciding what my next pose should be. When I'm finally done, I press enter and watch the numbers turn from just numbers on the page into pretty graphs.

I lean back in the chair with a broad smile on my face as the graphs now represent a need for expansion of the casino and hotel. In less than twenty minutes, I just did what would take most people several hours to do.

"Here's your coffee," Tony says, entering the office with a coffee in each hand and sugar packets tucked under his arm.

I notice a small coffee stain on his shirt. *God, the man can't even get coffee without making a mess.*

"Thanks," I say.

I get out of the chair to allow Tony to have his seat back. I take one of the cups and add a sugar packet to it before drinking it. My eyes dart to Tony as I watch him stare at the screen.

"Holy shit!" Tony says. More coffee spills onto his lap from him being startled by the numbers on the screen. He covers his mouth when he realizes he swore in front of me. "I'm sorry, miss. I just...this is just...how did you do this?" Tony points to the screen.

"It's okay, Tony. I just rearranged one little thing. You did most of the work," I say.

"I need to get this to Mr. Browne right away." He hits print, and the paper begins shooting out of the printer next to the computer. He grabs the paper and moves quickly to the doorway. He pauses at the doorway and turns to me. "Come on, Ms. Felton. You need to take some of the credit with me."

I shake my head. "No, I didn't do anything that you wouldn't have been able to figure out on your own."

Tony shakes his head. "I've been working on this all week. I would never have reached this conclusion without you. Plus, you should meet Mr. Browne. Word is, he is in the running to take over your father's position."

I blush when he speaks about Killian. "We've already met."

A wicked smile forms on Tony's face as his eyebrows rise deliberately. "Ah, Mr. Browne is a very good-looking man."

I stare at Tony in disbelief. He did not just accuse me of being attracted to Killian. "I am not attracted to him," I say, answering a question that was never asked. "I'm just not a big fan of Killian. He's cocky and self-centered and..."

"You don't have to convince me of those things, Ms. Felton."

Great, now, we are back to Ms. Felton.

"I have worked for Mr. Browne for the past three years. He is all of those things, but he is also a good man. Give him a chance before you dismiss him."

I swallow hard and nod even though I don't agree with him. I don't want to give Killian a chance. I already did, and instead of being honest with me, he played with my emotions just because he could. A man like that doesn't deserve second chances.

I just don't know why all the men in my life keep pushing me to be with Killian. My father is pushing me, even in death. My grandfather is, and now Tony. *Don't they trust me to find my own man? To find someone better than Killian?*

Tony moves his head to the side, indicating for me to follow him, so I do.

I bite my lip as I watch Tony knock on Killian's door. *Please don't be here.*

"Come in," Killian shouts from inside.

Tony gives me a knowing smile before he pushes the door open and enters Killian's larger office. I enter slowly behind Tony, keeping my eyes down. Maybe Killian won't notice I'm here if I don't say anything and don't look at him.

"I have those numbers for you," Tony says.

"Thank you," Killian says. "I..." He pauses.

I know he's spotted me. I let my eyes drift up, and there he is, staring at me with the same intense eyes. He's wearing another dark suit, and another grim frown covers his face.

I try to move. I try to say something to make this less awkward. I can't though. It's like his eyes have captured me and glued me in place. I lose all my thoughts when I see him, except for how it felt to have his lips pressed against mine. I think about how it warmed me to see him smiling at me and no one else, something I realize he rarely does. I think about how it felt when his tongue finally touched me *there*, and I already feel desire forming deep in my belly from just thinking about it.

I blush. That's when I notice Killian's reactions change. It's just slightly. I notice, but it's not enough for Tony to notice. Killian's eyes turn from intense glaring to intense lust, and his lip curls up slightly into the tiniest of smiles at my reaction. *He knows.* He knows what dirty thoughts I'm thinking about, making me blush more.

Tony chuckles and shakes his head as he looks from me to Killian.

Killian glares at Tony. "What's so funny?"

"Nothing. Nothing's funny. I just think Robert is smiling down right now, seeing the two of you together."

"There is nothing going on," Killian and I both say in unison.

This makes Tony chuckle again. "Not yet." He winks at me. He takes a step closer to Killian. "Anyway, I have another call I need to get to. Have a look at the numbers. I think we finally have the data you need to present tomorrow to get the expansion you and Robert wanted."

I watch as Tony leaves, leaving me alone with Killian. I turn to go as well.

"Wait..." Killian says.

I don't know why, but I wait. When I turn back to him, his mouth has dropped open slightly as he stares at the papers in his hand.

"These numbers...they actually work," Killian says. He runs his hand through his hair. "How did he do it?" he asks himself. Forgetting I'm there, he begins typing on the computer again. "This is genius."

I smile. *Good for Tony.* I take another step, but the heel of my shoe clicks along the floor, bringing Killian's attention back to me.

Killian stands then and walks until he is blocking my exit. "How did he do this?" He holds up the papers.

I try to scrunch my face in a quizzical look, like I have no idea why Tony wouldn't be competent at his job. But again, I make a terrible actress, a terrible liar. I shrug and look down, avoiding Killian's eye contact.

His hand lifts my chin until I'm staring back at him as he furrows his eyebrows, searching my face for the answer.

"Who did this?" he says slowly while holding the papers up.

"Tony," I say quietly.

He shakes his head. "Tony sucks at numbers. He couldn't have done this, not even by accident." He moves his body closer to mine so that we are almost touching. "Who did this?"

"I don't know." My voice is shaky.

I don't know why he cares who did it. Killian moves closer, and I take a step back, unable to hold my ground any longer, but he grabs my elbow, holding me in place and keeping our bodies pressed together. I can feel his body breathing slow and easy against my chest, compared with my fast, quick breaths. I even think I feel his heart beating in his chest in a perfect, steady rhythm, unlike my now erratic heartbeat. He's not affected by my body, like I am by his. It disappoints me.

He raises his eyebrows at me. His lips graze mine, and I stop breathing.

"Who did this?"

I close my eyes. "Me."

I feel him suck in a breath. It wasn't what he had expected. When I finally open my eyes, he's gone. He's back at his desk, looking everything over again, like he must have missed a mistake. If I created this, it must be wrong.

"What are you doing?" I ask when I have caught my breath again.

"How did you know how to do this?"

I roll my eyes. I hate that he just answered my question with another question.

"It's not that hard. I just took the data Tony had and started over. When it was organized, it was obvious to see the trends over the last six months. But based on the numbers, you should add a thousand rooms to the expansion, not five hundred. It's a waste of money to do such a small expansion. You'll reach positive cash flow faster with one thousand. It's sustainable in the long-term, too, even without the holiday spikes. And one good holiday season would more than triple sales with the additional guests staying in the hotel. So, the casino expansion looks spot-on with the data."

Killian is frowning at me. I nervously run my hand through my hair as I bite my lip. I should have kept my mouth shut. He thinks I'm wrong. He thinks I'm an idiot.

"What was your major in college?"

I narrow my eyes. "You already know the answer to that."

He raises his eyebrows though, waiting for me to answer.

"Theater," I say.

He nods. "You didn't take any business classes on the side? You didn't minor in anything?"

"I minored in French, but I didn't take any business classes."

Killian cocks his head to the side, trying to decide if I'm lying. I'm not.

"What jobs have you done, other than modeling?"

I have no idea where he is going with this. "I've only ever modeled."

"I don't know how you did this." He shakes head before running his hand through his locks. "I spent all morning working on the numbers. I knew whatever Tony gave me would be useless."

I sigh. I wish I had known that before. I wouldn't have worked so hard to try to save his ass.

"But I never came up with these numbers. I never came up with anything half as good as this."

I smile.

"You're a walking contradiction, princess."

My face falls. "Don't call me that."

He stands and walks over to me. "I can't stop, princess. That's what you are. It feels weird to call you anything else."

I glare at him, but I'm not really angry, so I know it doesn't come across as the angry girl I want to be.

"I want you," he says when his body is close to me again.

I quizzically look up at him. "You want to marry me?"

He laughs. "No, I want to fuck you."

I stare at him, wide-eyed. I don't move as his lips come down on mine, showing me just how much he wants to fuck me. His hands find the nape of my neck, firmly holding me against him. I moan as his tongue sweeps between my lips, easily parting them. I feel his hard erection pushing against my belly.

Does he expect me to fuck him right here in his office?

Killian pulls away, but I don't open my eyes. I'm still lost in that kiss. When I open my eyes, I'll realize this is all a dream. He's just toying with my emotions again. He doesn't care about me. He might want to fuck me, but only so he can destroy me.

"You're not ready yet."

"Ready for what?"

"For me to fuck you. I told you, when I fuck you, it will be because you want me as much as I want you, not because you're running. You're not there yet, but you will be."

I shake my head. "You're wrong. What makes you think I will sleep with you? I don't even like you."

He smirks. "You're a terrible liar, princess. Plus, if you are talking to Tony about me, that's a good sign."

"Tony needs to mind his own business."

He turns away from me to walk back to his desk. "You need to stay out of the business. Go home to your comfy house and modeling career before you get hurt."

"What is that supposed to mean? I am capable of running this company, if that's what I decide I want. I just showed I could make decisions and run numbers. I just need a chance."

He sits in his chair and stares at me for several minutes. I don't know why I bother with trying to convince him that I can do this.

"Okay," he says.

"What?"

"Okay, if you think you can do this, then prove it. There is a meeting tomorrow afternoon to present the data and to give my recommendation for the expansion. You can present in my place. And if you convince everyone you are right; then I'll stop hounding you about giving up. I'll even help you get up to speed on everything with the company."

I suspiciously eye him. "And what if I don't?"

He smiles widely now. I'm afraid he's going to tell me I'll have to stop trying to be CEO, that I'll have to give up. I'm not sure I can.

"Then, you go on a date with me."

I relax. I can handle that. "Deal."

"Good, I'll send you my notes for the meeting."

"Thanks," I say before turning to leave. But before I do, I have one more question for him, one that's been gnawing at me. "Why haven't you fired Tony yet?"

He looks up at me, like I'm crazy.

"We both know he is terrible at his job. So, why haven't you fired him?"

"Because I respect his loyalty. That man would take a bullet for this company. I know I'm going to have to work harder to do things, like create graphs he should be doing, but that's okay. He cares, and he is a hard worker. He would never jump ship to a competitor's company. We need more people like him around here."

His words shock me. I thought Killian was ruthless. I thought he would have fired Tony the second my father died since the decision was now up to him. I was wrong. It makes me wonder what else I'm wrong about when it comes to Killian. Too bad I don't have time to find out.

I need to spend the next twenty-four hours doing everything to prepare for tomorrow. I need to impress the other executives. I need to prove to my grandfather I can do this. I need to prove to myself this is what I want. It might be my only chance.

9

I move my hand to rub my eyes, but I stop myself. If I rub my eyes, I will ruin my mascara. I yawn instead, the exhaustion getting to me. It will be worth it though when I see Killian's smug face turn into one of his classic frowns when I win. I have no doubt I will. I've been up all night, going over everything Killian sent me along with seeing if there is any more data I need to prove my recommendation.

I was surprised actually when I got the email from Killian. He sent me everything he had on the project, including his personal notes and email exchanges between him and my father. Those were hard to read, but I read them anyway. He sent me hours and hours of material. I don't know why he would do that if he wanted me to fail. Maybe he wants me to succeed.

"Ready?" Killian says as he pokes his head into my father's office.

"Yes," I say.

I gather my things and follow Killian. I do my best to stand tall and confident even though everything inside is trembling. I follow Killian until we get to the conference room where the meeting is going to be held.

"You'll do great," he says, winking at me, before he holds the door open for me.

I walk in, but I have no idea what he is doing. *Is he trying to give me fake confidence? Is he trying to distract me?* I have no idea. I push the thoughts from my head and instead walk into the room with an intense expression on my face. I try to pretend I'm Killian walking into the room. He wouldn't be smiling and happy. He would be glaring at everyone, forcing them to do what he said with just one look.

I can't keep the expression up long though as I walk in. I'm a little in shock at the number of people in this room. There is close to thirty, and the room isn't even filled yet. I was expecting to present to a small intimate team of ten people, max. Instead, I'm going to be presenting to what feels like the entire company.

Killian puts his hand at the small of my back, guiding me to the front of the long table in the center of the room that has at least ten chairs around it. Those are probably for the most important people. On either side of the table, there are three rows of chairs holding at least ten more people, and they are all staring at me.

"Killian, why didn't you tell me there was going to be so many people at this meeting? Who are they?" I hiss between clenched teeth.

He smiles brightly. "I didn't want you to be nervous, but no need to worry. You'll do great. You are completely prepared. The main table here is the execs, which is where you will need to focus most of your attention when you talk. The rest are their assistants and staff who will be in charge of helping to implement the expansion. They might have a few questions for you because they are more familiar with what the day-to-day operations will look like."

I stare, wide-eyed, until we get to the end of the table where we each take a seat. I realize now why he's being so nice to me. It's not because he wants me to do well. It's because he has fed me to the wolves, and I'm about to get slaughtered.

I've never given a speech in front of this many people. The only thing I have done in front of this many people is model, and all that involved was looking pretty while walking down a catwalk without falling. It was nothing compared with this.

Killian leans over to me. "You wanted a chance. I'm giving you a chance. This is what it's really like to run the company."

He grabs my hand and gives it a quick squeeze before he stands. It does nothing to reassure me. Instead, I feel my palm growing sweaty from where he just touched it.

"I'm Killian Browne, VP of Operations. Today, I'm supposed to present the plans for the expansion of the Felton Grand. I'm not going to do that." He pauses while people uncomfortably shuffle in their seats at his statement. "Instead, I'm going to let the person who ran the data explain. I would like to introduce you to Kinsley Felton."

I stop bouncing my foot under the table and stand. The room has fallen silent now that they know Robert's daughter is the one who will be speaking. I smile weakly around the room as I get up from my chair. Killian winks at me again before taking a seat.

"Hi. I'm Kinsley." I can feel my heart beating out of my chest with every word I'm saying. "Today, I would like to show you my thoughts on the expansion and what the data shows." I walk to the computer that is already set up with my slides. I press the button for them to turn to the first screen.

I realize I've been staring at the ground the whole time, so I look up. Dozens of eyes fall on me, but to my surprise, all the faces are smiling. A few of them are trying to check out what's underneath my pencil skirt and pale pink shirt, but for the most part, I'm getting friendly faces in return. *I can do this.*

"As you can see from the graph, the numbers show a steady increase from month to month in the hotel and casino revenue. This shows there is a need for expansion because we can't keep up with the demand."

I continue talking, uninterrupted, for thirty minutes, explaining every reason we should do the expansion and why it is in the best interest of the entire company. I feel good about my presentation. It seems to be going well, and everyone is giving me their undivided attention. I even glance over at Killian a couple of times, and he seems to be nodding his head in approval.

I click the computer to get it to move to the last slide, the one where I give my recommendation. I feel good throughout my speech. Maybe I can do this. Maybe this is where I belong. "After looking at all the data, it is my recommendation that we increase the expansion to one thousand rooms. That would also allow us to increase the number of slots and the high-roller rooms by fifty percent. It..." I don't continue though. As I glance around the room, there are about a hundred hands in the air. At least, that's what it looks like.

"Yes," I say, pointing to the closest gentleman at the center table.

"I'm sorry, but it would be ridiculous to spend that amount of money on an expansion where we will never get our money back out of it. If we put those kinds of resources behind the Felton Grand, we aren't going to have enough resources to keep the others from failing."

I freeze at his question. "I, um...I'm not sure."

I point to the next man, hoping he will say something positive to save me.

"The data you used doesn't make sense with the data we already have. I just went through the numbers again. They don't line up. Can you explain why we have different numbers?"

"I don't know."

"What metrics did you use?" another man says.

"I...I'm not sure." I have no idea what he is talking about, and I can feel my face getting redder. I try to gather myself. "If you would just turn your attention to this slide, I can better explain to give you more confidence in the plan."

"Wouldn't expanding to just five hundred give us the same amount of profit in just a month longer with less risk?"

"Maybe, but—"

"Then, why don't we just do the five-hundred-room expansion?"

"I—"

"Killian, why have the plans changed?" a man sitting less than five seats from me asks.

Shit, now, they are addressing Killian instead of me.

"Killian, I think you'd better finish the presentation," Granddad says.

I didn't even realize he was in the room. I'd thought if he heard how great of a job I did from others, he would believe I could do this. Instead, I've just fucked up, proving him right.

I swallow before nodding at Killian to finish. He seems

reluctant to get up, but he does. I brush past him as I walk. I walk past all the stares. I walk past all the embarrassing murmurs. I walk out of the room until I find my father's office.

I fall onto my father's couch, and then I cry.

I've failed.

I can't do this.

I was wrong to even try.

Killian knew that. My grandfather knew that. Even my father knew that. They all knew I wasn't strong enough to handle this.

I should just marry Killian. Or better yet, I should just let him have the company. I could go back to modeling where nobody ever asked me any questions that were difficult. Instead, I got praise daily for how beautiful I was. I felt important. Now, I feel broken.

"What were you thinking?" Granddad says.

I sit up and wipe my tears. "I just wanted to prove I could do it. That I could be a part of the company and not just sit on the sidelines while Killian runs it. I want to be more than a trophy wife."

He sighs before walking over to me and taking a seat next to me. "I know you do, but you have to know your strengths. That doesn't include giving big speeches or making decisions. Your beauty is your strength. If you want to help and be a part of the company, then agree to do some modeling for our ads. Be the face of the company, not the voice."

"But I want more. I want to be more than just a pretty face."

"You don't need to be though. You're beautiful. You have a perfect life. There is no need to throw that all away just to try to feel more useful. If you're not careful, Killian won't even want to marry you, and then you'll be out of luck. I'm afraid I'll have to make that man CEO whether he marries you or not. He's too good at his job to let him go to our competition."

He stands. "If you were smart, you would be focusing on getting him to fall for you instead of thinking of how you can be more useful to the company. You are most useful as Killian's wife. You need him to fall in love with you before he figures out I will promote him whether he marries you or not."

I watch my grandfather as he walks out of my father's office without saying another word. Killian already knows he's invaluable to the company. He already knows he will become CEO whether or not he marries me. That's why he proposed what he proposed.

Maybe my grandfather's right. I should be focused on getting Killian to fall in love with me instead of focusing on getting my grandfather to believe I can do this.

"I figured you would be in here," Killian says.

"Do you ever knock?"

"No. You find out the best stuff if you don't knock."

I do my best to casually wipe my eyes, so he doesn't think I've been sitting here, crying, but it's no use. He knows that's what I've been doing.

"Here to gloat?"

He narrows his eyes. "No, I figured you would be the one who was going to do the gloating."

"Why would I do that? I failed. I lose. You win."

He smiles. "I would call it more of a tie."

I watch as he walks over and casually takes a seat on the sofa.

"What do you mean, we tied? I did horrible in there. They were practically laughing at my plan."

"I wouldn't say that. They ended up agreeing with you in the end."

"What? How?"

He sighs. "I should have told you there was pushback for even doing the smaller expansion in the first place. Nobody wanted to do it. There was no way you were going to convince them we should spend that kind of money and take that kind of risk, no matter what the data said."

"You did! It took you less than twenty minutes to convince them!"

"Ten actually," he says, smirking.

I hit him with a throw pillow.

"Sorry, just thought you should know it was a joint effort. You supplied the information and got them warmed up. I just closed the deal."

I roll my eyes. "No, you win. I didn't close the deal, as you say. I couldn't even answer their simple questions."

His smile widens. "I was happy just to call it a tie, but if you want to go on a date with me that badly, you can just ask."

I roll my eyes for a second time. "So, what happened after I left?"

He shrugs. "I answered their questions and told them it was happening whether they wanted it to or not, and it would be better if the company as a whole were behind it."

I frown when he puts his arm around me, but I admit it does relax me a little to have it there.

"Who has the ultimate decision then about if the expansion will go on or not?"

"Right now, your grandfather."

I nod, realizing the only reason they even had a meeting with half of the company was to get them behind the decision. It was never for them to decide the fate of the company. My grandfather was always the one who was going to make that decision. If I had just gone straight to him with my speech, maybe things would have been different. Maybe then, he would have realized I was more than just a pretty face. *Too late now.*

"So, when is this date I have to go on?" I sigh.

He tucks a loose strand of hair behind my ear. His touch sends chills down my arms.

"You are eager."

"No," I say, shaking off the chills. "Just ready for it to be over."

"Tomorrow, then."

I nod although I have no idea why I agreed to go out with him. All he wants is another chance to fuck me. I don't plan on giving him that pleasure, but as his eyes travel over my body, stopping at my chest, I don't know if I'll be able to resist his temptation.

Maybe fucking him is the only way to get over him?

10

———

Killian is late, thirty minutes late. He hasn't called. He hasn't texted. Nothing.

I pace back and forth in the living room of my new room that feels more like an apartment than a hotel room. It's the presidential room. It's the room Dad and I would stay in when we stayed at the hotel.

I had most of my stuff moved into the hotel this morning. I couldn't live in the family house any longer. I like living by myself. And hotel rooms feel more like home than my own house ever will. It will also help to be closer to the offices below. If I'm still committed to figuring out how to convince my grandfather I can do this job, then I need to learn from everyone in the casino—from the maids to the card dealers to the managers. I need all the help I can get to learn this business.

And if I'm honest with myself, I didn't want Killian picking me up from my parents' house. I wanted a place of my own, however temporary.

I pace again. I should have had Scarlett stay. She would have known what to do when he didn't show up. I should call her and tell her to come back, that we should just have a girls' night instead.

I hear a knock on the door. I open the door, and my jaw drops. Killian is standing there. That, I expected. What I didn't expect to see was him dressed so casually. He's in dark jeans and a T-shirt. His hair isn't gelled like usual. Actually, it looks a little unkempt. And a five o'clock shadow completes his look.

He grins at me when he sees my expression. I look down at how I'm dressed. *Shit!* I'm in a dress, a nice dress. I was expecting formal Killian. All I've ever seen him in is suits. I thought that's what he would wear since he came straight from work to pick me up. He's not.

"What's wrong, princess?" he asks smugly.

"I need to change," I say. I turn to run back into my bedroom to change.

He grabs my arm. "No time. My meeting ran late."

"You should have called and let me know you were going to be late."

"I should have, but I'm an asshole. And I like seeing you squirm."

He pulls me into the hallway, and I hear the hotel door shut behind me before I can protest. We enter the elevator, and he presses the button for the ground floor. I can't look at him. I'm too embarrassed.

Scarlett helped me decide what to wear. She told me to wear this black, slightly see-through, lace dress, so I did. I shouldn't have.

"I like your hair like this." His thumb caresses my exposed neck, thanks to Scarlett for putting my hair up.

I quickly forget why I'm supposed to be embarrassed when he is looking at me like this. I lick my bottom lip, preparing for the kiss that always follows that look.

"I like that it gives me better access to your neck." He softly kisses me on my neck but doesn't do anything further.

Instead, he grabs my hand, and when the doors open, we walk out of the elevator and onto the casino floor. I let go of his hand as we walk through the casino. Several employees nod their heads at us in recognition—except they don't recognize me. They are acknowledging Killian. I'm surprised to see a smile on most of their faces when they see him. They seem to like him. He's probably a good boss, firm yet fair. I might be making a huge mistake, trying to take that away from the company, but I'm not trying to take it away. I'm just trying to improve upon that—whether that's with me or someone else.

We exit the casino into the warm Vegas air. Killian comes to an abrupt stop. I expect him to have changed his mind. I expect him to decide we should spend the whole date back in my hotel room or go to his place, wherever that is.

"I should have let you change. Can you walk in those?" He points to my black high heels.

"Yes, I can walk just fine in these." I'm surprised that he didn't order a car.

He raises his eyebrow. "You couldn't walk in them the other night."

"I had too much to drink that night. Trust me; I'll be fine. I've walked enough catwalks with heels twice as high and tighter dresses than this, all while being blasted with flashing lights. I'll be fine." The first part isn't true. I didn't have too much to drink that night. My body was just reacting to Killian's stare as he walked me to his hotel room that night.

It's the same stare he has on his face again as his eyes

travel over my body before landing on my black bra that is visible beneath my dress.

"What are you doing?"

"Trying to imagine you with fewer clothes or tighter clothes. I can't imagine it. I'm going to need a show later."

"This was a mistake."

I turn to go back to my room, but he stops me.

"I'm kidding. Relax, princess." He breathes slowly in and out, trying to get me to imitate him.

I roll my eyes at him.

"I'm just trying to make you smile, and apparently, I'm doing a terrible job. I'm a bit out of practice." His eyes stay transfixed on mine.

I laugh. *This guy is unbelievable.*

His lips curl up slightly at the sight of me laughing. He looks around to find the cause of my laughter. "What's so funny?"

"You are. You don't expect me to believe you haven't taken a different girl out every night. I bet you have had a different model or actress or showgirl in your bed every night this week." I raise my eyebrows at him, waiting for an answer.

"I don't date. At least, I haven't in a long time. Yes, I occasionally take a woman home to my bed, but even that happens rarely."

"Define *rarely.*"

He shrugs. "Once a quarter. Lately, less than that."

My eyes widen at his response, but I'm not sure I believe him.

"You are telling me you only sleep with a woman once a quarter or less?"

"Yes, I only fuck once a quarter or sometimes less."

I wince again when he says *fuck* although it's less apparent this time. That was not what I had expected.

"Why? You could have any woman you want on any night you want. You're good-looking and intelligent. You make more money than ninety-nine percent of the population. Sure, you act like a cocky ass most of the time, but your looks more than make up for it." I stop talking when I realize I'm rambling about all of Killian's qualities. This is the opposite of flirting. I should just shut my mouth.

He smugly takes my hand back in his. "Come on; we have a long walk ahead if you are wearing those shoes. And I want to get to dinner on time."

I sigh and go with him. "Why?" I ask again.

He pulls me around a group of people dressed up like the band Kiss. They are followed by a woman who's dressed up as Dolly Parton.

I relax a little though because I'm sure, wherever we are going, I'll be dressed appropriately. Vegas isn't known for its tame looks. People wear whatever they want to wear here, no matter where they are going.

"Just not interested in more than that, and women always want more after I fuck them. At night, they promise they don't want anything more than one night, but the next morning, they are begging to go out again. I hate having to fend them off. Once every couple of months is the max I can handle."

"Why haven't you found *the one* yet? I'm sure you want to settle down and get married. Most people your age have been married for years with several kids, old man."

He glares at me. "Just how old do you think I am?"

I shrug. "I don't know."

"I'm thirty. Thirty isn't old."

I smile. "It is to me."

He sighs. "God, you're such a child."

I feel his grasp on my hand loosen. I frown. I want him to hold my hand tighter. I want him to want me. I don't like him thinking about me as a child...except I shouldn't want him to want me. I shouldn't even be on this date.

"So, when is the last time you went on a date before tonight?"

Killian doesn't look at me when he answers, "Three years."

My jaw drops. "Three years? That's a long time." It's also the same time my father told him he wanted Killian to marry me. *Coincidence?* I don't know, but I'm too afraid to ask.

"When is the last time you went on a date?"

Eli, my high school boyfriend, was the last person I went on a date with. We dated for one year in college before he broke it off.

"It was...three years ago," I say as I realize it.

I stare up at him, and we stop walking.

He's looking at me like he wants to ask me the same question I want to ask him.

Did I stop dating because of him? I didn't—well, not exactly. I didn't know he existed yet. I didn't know my father had already chosen. I just knew it would eventually happen.

When I don't ask and when he doesn't answer, he turns us to the building we have stopped in front of.

"We are here."

Now, I really wish I had changed.

"What can I get you to drink?" the waitress says.

She looks tired, but when she looks down at my attire, I swear, she smirks at me.

I stare back down at the menu, hoping to God some drink will pop out at me so I will know what to order, but there are no drinks listed on the menu. I glance around the diner. From the looks of this place, I doubt they have the wine he's bought me before. Actually, I doubt they have any wine. I should order a beer, but I don't even know where to start. So, instead of answering the woman, I stare intently at my menu.

"What do you want to drink, Kinsley?"

I look up to see Killian staring at me with a small smile tugging at the corner of his lips. It's weird to hear my name fall from his lips. I can't recall him using it before, but I realize what he's doing. He's giving me exactly what I said I wanted. He's not going to help me, not unless I beg. And I'm not above begging right now if he will help me.

I plead with my eyes for him to just order a drink for us. I pucker my lip, like Scarlett taught me.

He rolls his eyes at my look and sits up straighter, turning his attention to the waitress.

"I'll have a Miller Lite. Bring her a Blue Moon. We will have your mountain onion ring appetizer with extra sauce. And we both want your special burger, hold the onions."

Killian takes the menu from me and hands it to the lady, who rushes off, glad to finally be done with us.

"You really can't make a quick decision."

"I can." I take a deep breath, ready to reveal something embarrassing. "I just haven't had a lot of experience with drinking. I've only drunk a handful of times in my life."

"Well, that explains a lot."

"You didn't have to order my dinner for me though."

"I was afraid if you took any longer, the waitress would

end up spitting in our food. She's obviously swamped tonight, and you were taking half an hour just to order your drink. What did you want? I'll make sure she changes the order."

I sigh. "I was going to order exactly what you ordered me." My cheeks flush at the admission that he was right —again.

Killian smiles and shakes his head.

"So, what made you choose this place? I'm guessing you don't come here often. Doesn't seem like it has the healthiest of menus."

"Just wanted to get you the best burger in Vegas after I almost denied you one the other day."

You denied me more than just a burger, I think as I bite my lip.

The beers and appetizer are thrust onto the table. I take a sip of the beer. It's definitely not the Chateau Margaux wine that Killian ordered me before, but it's drinkable. I take an onion ring off the tower before me.

"Tell me something about yourself. You might be my future husband one day, if we don't figure a way out of this mess. I might as well know more about you."

He shakes his head. "I've already figured a way out of this. You have yet to agree to it. But, okay, I'll play. What do you want to know?"

I take a bite as I contemplate what I want to know most. I really want to know what it would be like to be fucked by him. But I can't go there. I fidget with the wrapper on the silverware, trying to think of a tame question.

"Where did you go to college?"

"Yale."

"Really?"

"No," he says, laughing. "I went to Harvard. I majored in

business and then started law school there, but I didn't finish. Instead, Felton Corporation snatched me up, and I've been working here ever since."

"Did you grow up in Vegas?"

"Yes."

Hmm, that surprises me.

"What about you? Why Yale? Why theater?"

I take a long sip of my beer. I don't want to answer that. Instead, I try his trick. "What part of Vegas?"

"No, it's your turn. I answered your question. Now, you answer mine. That's how the game works."

"This isn't a game."

"Whatever, I'm not answering any more questions until you answer me. Why Yale? Why theater?"

I take another sip of my beer, stalling for as long as I can until I can't anymore. His stare pierces through me, forcing me to let go of whatever I'm hiding.

"My father. He chose Yale for me. He chose the theater major. I haven't chosen anything that's important in my life. Nothing of this life is mine."

"Why?"

I pause for just a second before I answer, "Because I loved him and could never disappoint him. Because family comes before everything."

There's a long pause as he lets my words sink in. He finally has the tiniest understanding of what my life is really like. Although if he was around my dad as much as he said, he already knew. He just wanted to hear it from me.

"I'm sorry."

I quizzically look at him.

"I'm sorry your life has never been your own."

I shrug as I keep back tears threatening to fall. "It's okay. It's been a good life."

His eyes are intense, as intense as I think I've ever seen them, as he says the next words, "But it's not *your* life. That's what I'm trying to give you—a chance to find your own life."

"What makes you think I want that?" I let my eyes drift to my lap as I tuck a fallen curl behind my ear.

"Because I do."

My eyes immediately go back to his. I don't know if he meant he wants that for me or he wants that for himself. But I feel like he just poured his heart out to me while sitting in a grungy diner.

"Two specials," our waitress snaps as she thrusts two plates of the biggest burgers I have ever seen in front of us.

When I glance back up at Killian, the moment is gone. It's passed. It doesn't keep me from wondering what Killian is hiding as I dig into my burger.

11

"I can't believe you ate that entire thing," Killian says while knocking on a hotel door.

"I was hungry, and that was delicious. I can't believe you didn't eat the entire thing."

He scrunches his face in disgust. "It was a pile of grease. We will probably both be sick tomorrow because of it."

I laugh. He's way too serious to relax. I bet he eats every nutrient his body needs and nothing more.

"What are we doing here?" I ask.

But I'm too late. The door opens, and a man slaps Killian on the back.

"Kill, you made it!" The man glances to me and then back to Killian. "Who is this?" he asks Killian while staring at me.

"This is my date for tonight, Kinsley."

I notice Killian intentionally leaves off my last name.

I appreciate it. Enough people in this town know my name I don't want to be stereotyped before this person even gets to know me.

"Kinsley, this is Grant Brampton, my best friend and one of the best poker players west of the Mississippi."

Grant tips his hat as Killian talks, making me giggle. He takes my hand and softly kisses it, eyeing Killian. I laugh harder as I notice Killian glaring at Grant. He knows exactly what he is doing—pissing Killian off. I like Grant already.

"Come in. The game is about to start," Grant says.

I follow Killian into the hotel room, except this room has been turned into a makeshift poker room. There is a large circular table in the center with decks of cards and chips stacked perfectly on one end. The kitchen has been turned into a mini bar. I notice three other men standing around with drinks in their hands.

"Everyone, this is Kinsley," Killian says.

Everyone says, "Hey," back with obvious curious stares as to why Killian has brought a date to a boys' night.

I'm curious about that myself. My hands are shaking slightly. I'm beginning to feel more confident around Killian, but a roomful of guys I don't know makes me uneasy.

"Killian, I can go home. I didn't mean to intrude on boys' night."

"Nah, they don't care. They'll be happy to have someone good-looking to gawk at while I take all their money. Plus, if we didn't go out tonight, I'm not sure of the next night I'm available to go out."

My heart sinks a little at his words. There's not going to be a second date. Or if there is, it's going to be a long time from now.

"This is Stephen Mann. He's my brother-in-law."

I shake Stephen's hand. I didn't know Killian had a sister.

"And that's Marvin and Benny. They both suck at poker."

Marvin throws popcorn at Killian. Killian runs over and pretends to tackle Marvin. It's strange, seeing Killian like this—relaxed and playful. I know he's called me a walking contradiction, but I'm beginning to see him the same way. He's serious and stern, one minute, and then playful and joking, the next.

"All right, settle, you two," Grant says. "It's time for you to lose some money." He pulls up another seat. "You can sit here," he says to me, holding on to the chair he just pulled up to the table.

"Thanks," I say, smiling, as I take a seat. I fold my hands in my lap to keep them from shaking.

Grant takes a seat on my left as Killian takes a seat on my right. All of the other men take their seats in the remaining chairs.

Marvin starts distributing chips to everyone in equal measure. When he gets to me, he asks, "You in?"

I glance to Killian, but he doesn't say anything. I notice his shoulders tense a little, but I think he would have said something if he didn't want me to play.

"Sure," I say.

"It's a hundred dollar minimum bet. Are you sure?" Marvin says.

I smile politely. "I'm sure."

"We will make Killian pay up when she loses," Grant jokes.

I want to tell Grant he's wrong, that I don't intend to lose, but I can't. I haven't played poker in years, and I'm a terrible liar. Father always used to say poker isn't about bluffing or telling the truth. It is about strategy and numbers. It's about knowing your odds. It's that simple.

Grant smiles at me. Marvin starts dealing out cards to everyone.

Killian leans over to whisper in my ear, "Do you know how to play Texas Hold 'em?"

"I know the basics. I'm sure I'll be fine."

I glance at my cards and wait for my turn. I quickly calculate my outs and odds. When it gets to me, I call. I have a thirty-five percent chance of winning, and the pot odds are thirty percent.

All the men call the initial hundred-dollar bet.

"What do you do, Kinsley?" Grant asks me.

I watch the initial flop. I get another nine to match my pair of nines. I want to smile, but I don't. I try to keep my emotions as neutral as possible as I begin counting my outs and odds again.

I answer Grant the only way I know how, "I'm a model."

"Oh, really?" Grant says, eyeing me. "I can see that. You definitely have the body for it."

Killian glares at Grant, but I can see it's just harmless fun. And, for whatever reason, I like Grant. He seems to know how to have a good time.

"She's more than that. She went to Yale," Killian says.

I'm surprised he is defending me.

I raise the bet on my turn, not by much though. It's just enough to only keep the serious players in the game. Benny folds on his next turn, but everyone else stays in.

"You're a pro player?" I ask Grant.

"Yep. I placed third in the World Series of Poker National Championship last year."

"Impressive," I say. I watch the next card played.

Another nine turns up, and I can't help but smile. I turn to Killian to pretend I'm smiling at him, but anybody that's paying me any attention would know why I'm smiling.

Grant is the only one paying me much attention though, and his eyes are on my chest, not my face.

I glance at Killian and see his face has grown dark. His eyes look like they are going to shoot lasers right through Grant.

I place my hand on Killian's thigh. "Relax," I whisper to him before shocking both of us by kissing him on the cheek. It's the most brazen I have been. I gently squeeze his leg, and I feel his muscles relax, if only a little, as I massage his thigh.

I keep my hand there long after he has relaxed. I like feeling his strong body beneath my hand. When I chance a glance down, I see a hint of an erection growing beneath his jeans. I have more control than I realize.

I smile. If I move my hand just an inch, I could accidentally touch it and then pretend I didn't mean to do it.

"Kinsley, what are you going to do?" Grant wakes me from my dream.

I quickly remove my hand. "I call."

Grant calls before he says, "The trick to poker is paying attention. It's math. It's knowing your odds and how to read people."

I smile at Grant trying to give me advice. I already know his hand isn't worth shit. His face says it all, yet he still thinks he's won with, most likely, a pair of face cards. And looking around the table, he probably would have.

Marvin flips his cards, showing high king, followed by Stephen with a pair of tens. Then, Killian flips over a straight, to my surprise. But it's still not enough. Grant nods for me to flip my cards over.

"Four of a kind," I say to Grant.

His smile drops as he flips over two aces, giving him three of a kind.

"I win," I say shyly. "I'll try to use your advice for the next hand though."

Marvin pushes the chips to me while Killian chuckles softly next to me.

"Did your father teach you how to play poker, too?" he asks in my ear so only I can hear.

I shrug and blush, and he chuckles again.

We play for another hour or so until the only players remaining are Killian, me, and Grant. I stay out of the conversation to my relief as the boys talk about sports and cars. I glance over at Killian. He won't stay in the game for much longer though. He's down to his last chips.

"How did you two meet?" Stephen asks as he brings me another beer.

I taste it, but it doesn't taste as good as the one Killian ordered earlier.

I glance nervously at Killian. I'm not ready to share our story, but I suck at lying and don't want to lie to a member of his family.

"We met three years ago."

I choke on my beer when Killian says that. *God, I've got to stop doing that.* I turn to face him, trying to decide if he's lying or telling the truth, but Killian has the best poker face I have ever seen.

"I was giving a speech to a business class at Yale. While I was there, I paid a visit to an old friend." He doesn't look at me when he says the next words, "Eli Stratford. You remember him, Grant. He was Charlie's younger brother."

"Yeah, I remember Charlie. I didn't know Eli that well though. I didn't know you were friends," Grant says.

Killian shakes his head. "We weren't really, but like I said, I presented in front of a business class, and Eli was there. He introduced himself afterward, and I agreed to meet him for lunch.

"Anyway, we were at lunch, and the most beautiful woman I had seen came walking into the restaurant. I considered leaving Eli alone right there, so I could go after the woman, but to my surprise, she walked over to our table and kissed Eli on the lips. Then, she asked for the keys to his apartment, so she could study there instead of walking back to hers across campus. And she left. That woman was Kinsley. She recently moved back into town after graduating, and I asked her out. And here we are."

Killian still won't look at me. Grant puts his arm around me, and I force a smile on my face.

"Too bad the old man here snatched you up, but if you want to have a good time, you'll go out with me sometime," Grant says, winking.

I smile. "I don't know if I can go out with someone who loses to me in poker."

"I haven't lost yet—unlike Killian who is about to get slaughtered."

Grant begins dealing the cards again, drawing his attention away from me. My thoughts stay on Killian though, even as the cards are dealt. I don't remember that story. I don't remember that happening, and it's quite an extravagant lie just to keep Grant away from the truth—that we are basically having an arranged marriage.

I glance at my cards. I call on my turn. I'm giving half of my attention to what Killian just said and the other half to the game at hand.

After we have all called, Grant flops the first three cards.

I quickly count my outs and then calculate my odds—fifty-five percent. It's greater than the pot odds. I double the bet on my turn.

Why in the hell did Killian tell that story? How did he know I was dating Eli?

Another card is turned over. My odds increase to sixty percent.

I look at Killian. I notice a tiny bead of sweat forming on his face. His leg is shaking under the table. He increases the bet again. *He's lying.*

But just moments ago, the only sign was him avoiding my gaze. That was the truth. Suddenly, I remember. I remember seeing a strange, hot man having lunch with Eli. I remember going back to Eli's apartment and studying before waiting for him to walk me to my afternoon class, like he always did—except, that day, I never made it to class. When Eli got home from that lunch, we got in the worst fight we had ever been in. Eli seemed to think I was already engaged to another man. That it would never work out with us. He broke up with me that night. *Killian was the one that told him I was engaged. Killian broke us up.*

"All in," I say, pushing the chips into the middle of the table.

I can't stay here any longer. I don't care about winning or losing anymore. I don't care about flirting with Killian anymore. I just want to get out of here.

I see the shock on Killian's and Grant's faces, but they both push their chips in. Grant flips the last card, and then I flip my cards over, despite it being out of turn.

"Royal flush." I glance right and then left when they both flip over their cards—a full house and a straight. "I win."

I push my chair back and get up. I walk out without a word. I can't breathe as I run down the hallway. It feels claustrophobic, like the walls are closing around me. I won't survive in an elevator, so I run down the stairs of the hotel building instead. I need to be moving. I need to get away from Killian.

If it wasn't for him, I could still be with Eli. I could have chosen my own love, my own future. Instead, Killian convinced Eli to break up with me. Instead, he chose my future for me.

12

THE AIR OUTSIDE is warm and just as stifling as it was inside the hotel room. I begin the long walk back to my hotel—alone. I could call a car to pick me up, but I don't. I prefer to be alone.

I make it a few steps before I look up and see Killian standing on the sidewalk, waiting for me. *Damn it!*

The elevators must be faster than climbing down five flights of stairs in heels. I can't walk around him. I can't avoid him. So, I just walk to him.

"What just happened?" he asks.

"Nothing. We're done. I don't want to be friends. I definitely don't want to marry you. And I don't want your help. I just want to go back to being nothing."

I begin walking again, and Killian falls in step next to me. He doesn't say a word for an entire block. He doesn't touch me either. Despite how much I hate him right now, my body is begging for him.

"I'm sorry," he finally says. "I'm sorry I didn't tell you the truth."

I glare at him. "What is the truth?"

"The story I gave during the poker game is the truth. I was giving a presentation to a class at Yale. I knew Eli a little bit from my past, not enough to really have lunch with him, but then the opportunity came up, and I took it.

I knew from your father you were dating him. I just wanted to learn more about you, to see if you were happy with Eli. If you were, I wouldn't approach you. I wouldn't say anything to Eli about your father's arrangement with me. But if you weren't happy...well, I wasn't sure what I was going to do.

"When you came into that restaurant that day, you looked sad, withdrawn. Even when you kissed him, it wasn't a kiss of passion. I couldn't let you waste the only few years of freedom you had left on that douchebag. So, I told him the truth. Well, I told him you and I were already engaged, and no matter what he did, you would never marry him."

"He broke up with me that night because of you." My face is fuming bright red.

"I only did it to help you find someone who would make you happy. I thought, if you were away from him, you would find someone else."

"But I didn't! I didn't find someone else. You ruined the only real relationship I ever had. You are just as bad as my father. You tried to control my life!"

He eyes widen, and his mouth drops.

We both stop walking.

"That was never my intention. I just wanted you to be happy, and I know you weren't happy with Eli."

"How do you know if I was happy or not? What right did you have to decide anything for me?"

"I know because you never smiled, not once the whole time you were around him, and you have smiled over a hundred times since you met me. I know because your eyes didn't lust after Eli, like they lust after me." He tucks a stray hair behind my ear. "I know because you are an amazing woman who deserves to be worshipped by the man she is with, and all Eli did that entire time was complain about how clingy and annoying you were."

"I'm not clingy."

"I know. Eli's an idiot. You shouldn't have dated him."

"So are you."

"You're right. I'm an idiot, too. You should have dated someone else. You should have moved on after Eli."

I shake my head. "I couldn't...I couldn't date when I knew it would never go anywhere, when I knew it would always leave me heartbroken, when I knew I was always meant to be with you...except I didn't know who you were yet because you never told me."

"I'm sorry."

"I'm sorry, too. You shouldn't be forced to marry me to get a position in the company you clearly deserve."

Killian intensely stares at me, trying to understand what I'm saying, but I don't know what I'm saying. I just want him to know this situation is completely fucked up.

All I know is, I still want him.

I moisten my lips, begging for his lips to find mine. They do. His lips sink into mine as his hands go around my body. I moan against his lips.

I forget about being on a busy sidewalk on the strip. I forget about how mad at him I still am for lying to me. I forget about how angry I am at him for manipulating my life.

I just kiss and moan and beg.

Killian's kiss is aggressive and hungry. He wants me as much as I want him. He needs this.

I don't think about the fact that, in a few months, we

could be walking down the aisle as man and wife, and having a one-night stand now could ruin it all. I don't care. I need him. I need to feel what it's like to have a man burying himself deep inside me as we both come.

We finished walking back to the hotel, kissing along the way, before I realize this is a bad idea. We can't walk into the hotel, kissing and holding hands. Everyone who works in the casino will see us and start rumors. Those rumors will get back to my grandfather, and he will assume we have decided to marry when that couldn't be further from the truth.

"Maybe we should go back to your place. I don't want any of the staff to see us together."

"This is my place." He releases my hand as soon as we get close to the entrance. "No one will suspect if we go up to our rooms together. Our rooms are right next door to each other."

"They are? You kept your room from the first night? Why do you live in a hotel room?"

"I feel more at home here. And having a hotel room here lets me be closer to work. I've had enough emergency calls I have had to tend to in the middle of the night that it's just easier to already be here."

I nod, understanding.

"Why do you live in a hotel when I know you have a home only a few minutes away?" he asks.

"I feel at home here. I've always felt at home in hotels. The mansion has never felt like home."

Killian smiles. "Your father used to say the same thing."

"Come on. This time, you take the stairs, and I'll take the elevator."

He laughs. "No, we will both take the elevator."

We walk into the casino, side by side, but we don't

touch. Employees notice us and nod in our direction. This time though, I feel like they can see the truth. They know we are walking upstairs to go have sex. They all know. It will be the talk of the town tomorrow.

My hand shakes nervously at my side, and I try my best to smile at a bartender as she walks by, but it's weak.

"Relax. No one suspects a thing," Killian whispers into my ear.

"Don't do that," I hiss. "It just makes us look more suspicious to see you talking into my ear."

We make it to the elevator without drawing too much attention to ourselves. When the doors close, the tension between us is too much to remain frozen and not touching. Our bodies collide. Our arms wrap around each other as our lips touch in one of the best kisses of my life. I don't know if it's the tension that caused this kiss to be even better than the rest, or maybe it's the underlying anger I feel toward him. Whatever the reason, I don't want it to stop.

The elevator dings, indicating we are stopping, that the doors are going to open soon, that we have to stop. But we can't. We are desperate for each other, desperate to hold on to whatever this fleeting feeling is. I'm sure, as soon as we have sex, it will be gone, and we will go back to being mortal enemies. But, for now, it lasts.

The doors open, and Killian tears his lips from mine just in time for the woman standing there to only suspect that we were kissing, but not long enough to have proof. I notice her smile knowingly anyway as our heavy panting gives away what we were just doing. She's not an employee though. The woman who enters the elevator has no idea who we are.

It doesn't keep me from flushing a bright shade of pink though. I've never been caught making out with a man before, not even in high school or early college when Eli and I were dating. We never did anything so risky to chance being caught.

The elevator dings again on the top floor, the floor both Killian and I have rooms on. Killian motions with his hand for me to step out first. So, I do, pushing any thoughts of Eli out of my mind. Tonight isn't about him. I'll deal with those memories later.

Tonight is about need and desire. Tonight is about me finally becoming a woman who can sleep with a man without becoming attached. Tonight is about giving in to my own desires without thoughts of the consequences. Tonight is about me. It's about fucking.

I make my way to my hotel door and slip the key card in. I watch the red light flick to green. I push the handle down, opening the door. Killian's body is quickly pushing me inside as soon as the latch on the door releases.

I let out a small whimper when he pushes me inside. I wasn't expecting him to move so quickly.

He claims my lips with his in a brutal, carnal kiss. It's a kiss that can't be mistaken for anything but what it is—a desperate plea for me to give myself to him. Fuck, when he kisses me like that, giving so much of himself to me, I want nothing more than to give him everything.

I try to match the hunger of his kiss with my own, but my inexperienced tongue gets tangled in his. His tongue takes back control. This time, I let him do what he wants, and I enjoy the way he molds us together with just his tongue.

Killian breaks away from my lips as his hand finds my hair and releases the clip holding it up. His eyes follow my curls as they bounce down my back. His hand tangles into my hair as his lips find mine again, deepening the kiss.

I moan as he tugs softly on my locks.

I've never been controlled by a man before. Eli is really my only experience other than Brent—if that could even be called a sexual experience. And Eli was always soft, gentle, thoughtful. He didn't have an aggressive bone in his body, not like this man attacking me with his body.

Killian's hand finds my ass, and he lifts me. I wrap my legs around his waist, feeling his hard body beneath me. He carries me to the bedroom. I moan from the movement of my already drenched pussy rubbing against him with every step.

He drops me on the bed before his eyes admire my body. I bite my lip as I watch his eyes take in my black bra and panties beneath my dress. For the first time tonight, I feel happy I chose this skimpy dress.

His eyes stay on my body as he slowly and deliberately removes my high heels. It's one of the sexiest things I've ever seen, but I know it will soon be replaced when he removes his clothes. When my shoes are off, I stand and turn around. I lift my hair off my neck.

Killian knows what I'm asking without me having to say a word. His hand finds the zipper, and he slowly pulls it down. I feel his hot breath on my neck the whole time, each exhale sending shivers down my spine.

I drop my hair, and he slowly turns me around until I'm facing him. He cups my chin in his hand, and his thumb softly strokes my cheek.

"I need to hear you say it."

His words are cryptic, but I know what he's asking. I try to make my eyes as lust-filled as possible when I look at him. I know, no matter what I say, my words won't be enough for him, if my body isn't saying the same thing. And I'm not going to let him get away with just letting his lips and tongue taste me. I want more. I'm desperate for his cock to be inside me. I'm desperate to feel what a real release feels like from a man experienced in giving me what I want.

"I want you," I say.

He takes a deep breath before pushing our bodies together. "Not good enough." His eyes have grown intense with burning need.

I moan as his lips brush against my neck, sending more chills throughout my body.

"I need you."

He shakes his head against my neck. "Not good enough."

His hand presses against my soaked panties covering my pussy.

"Fuck," I let out.

His lips smile just a little against my neck. His lips move back to mine as he slips one finger into my panties. My breath catches in my throat at his slow, torturous touch.

I can't *not* have him. I can't let him walk away from this. I'll die if he doesn't take me.

His lips along with his finger finally pull away from me. I whimper at the loss of his touch. I grab ahold of his neck and shoulders, barely able to stand. My breathing is fast, and my heartbeat is erratic. I do my best to catch my breath before I speak, but I can't.

I look into his hungry whiskey-colored eyes and say the dirtiest, most truthful thing that has ever escaped my lips, "Fuck me, Killian. Take me, own me, control me. I can't survive another second without knowing how your cock feels inside me."

His head cocks slightly as he smiles brighter than I've ever seen. "It will be my pleasure."

As soon as the words leave his mouth, his whole body

moves to another level. I didn't know another level of intensity could exist between two people. I was wrong.

My dress falls down my body as his shirt comes off. His pants fall quickly, and he steps out as he pushes me back onto the bed.

He kisses me now like I'm the only woman he ever wants to kiss, like I make him whole. And when he kisses me, I feel the same way. Not like I know I'm going to be left heartbroken after this. Our hands link together high over my head as his erection presses between my legs.

I feel my nipples growing hard beneath my bra, begging to be touched. He senses my need and releases my hands to unhook my bra. The cold air makes my nipples perk higher. He palms my breast with his hand as the ache grows in my swollen breasts. He finds my nipple and squeezes roughly.

"Fuck," I moan.

He smiles. "I think I like your dirty mouth."

"Fuck," I moan again. "Just don't stop."

I pant as he takes the next one in his hand and gives it the same attention he gave the first.

My pussy aches for attention as he presses harder against me. He senses that, too, and his hand releases one breast to sink down inside my panties. He finds my clit and rubs until I'm panting harder. I need him even more than before.

"Please," I beg.

His lips hover just above mine. "Please, what, princess?"

"Please, I need you inside me." My pussy aches harder, desperate to be filled.

He stands and pulls my panties off my body until I'm completely bare for him. He only takes a second to admire my body before picking up his discarded jeans, but it feels like his eyes soak me in for hours. I think, if I asked him, he could recall every curve, every freckle, and every imperfection of my skin. That's how well his eyes have taken in my body.

I watch as he pulls a condom out of his pocket. I try not to think why he would have one in his pocket in the first place, but my thoughts drift anyway. *Did he pick me up tonight with this intention? Or did he plan on picking up another random girl as soon as he dropped me off?*

The thoughts quickly float out of my head when he drops his boxers, and I watch his thick, hard cock spring free.

My breath catches at the sight. I have to touch it. I have to make him feel as good as he has made me feel.

"Touch it," he commands, reading my thoughts again.

I hesitantly reach my hand out to stroke him. He moans at my touch, giving me more confidence, and I tighten my grip around his straining erection. I move up and down, slow and steady.

"Fuck, princess," he moans.

I pick up speed, as his arousal somehow grows larger.

He suddenly grabs my wrist, and I stop the movement and look up at him with wide eyes.

"Enough," he says.

He rips the condom open with his mouth, an obviously practiced move. He easily slides it on, never taking his dangerous eyes off of mine. I sink back into the bed, climbing up further away from him. I feel my heartbeat race in anticipation of what is about to happen. I swallow hard, trying to push the nervous energy down, but it doesn't work. I can feel my heartbeat in my throat.

Killian climbs up the bed until he is on top of me. He kisses me hard and controlling as I feel him settle in between my legs again. I tremble slightly when he caresses my breast.

He looks up at me with troubled eyes. "Is this your first time, princess?"

"No," I whisper. But it might as well be. It's been three years. And even then, it only happened a handful of times, and none of them felt even a fraction as good as this has so far.

His eyes travel over my face, trying to understand the contradiction between my words and what my body is saying. He tucks a hair behind my ear, trying to calm my nerves. "I'm not going to hurt you, princess."

I nod, but I can't control my body. I can't keep it from reacting this way. When he realizes I'm not going to relax from just his words, he tries with his lips, with his tongue. His tongue sinks into my mouth, and I lose myself in his kiss.

His hand finds my clit again, and he works me into a frenzy of need. I moan as I grow closer. I'm so close to coming. My eyes open for just a second, and I see him giving me one final warning with his eyes before he sinks inside me.

"Fuck, Killian," I moan as he stretches me with his cock. I didn't even realize I could stretch that wide for him.

"You're beautiful, princess. Look at me," Killian says, taking me off the pain for a second.

When I do, I see the appreciation there. I moisten my lips moments before his lips join with mine again. I feel him sink further into me, but this time, my body welcomes the wince of pain because it knows it'll bring me closer to the pleasure about to ensue.

His hands lock back with mine, high over my head, as he gently rocks inside me. We both moan as he does. The pleasure begins to sweep over my body with each move-ment. His body moves slowly at first in a steady rhythm that my body easily matches.

His body quickly increases his rhythm, thrusting harder and faster. Each time his body presses into mine, another jolt of pleasure flows through every nerve ending in my body. Each thrust brings me closer and closer to exploding in ecstasy. Each thrust sweeps me further and further under his spell.

"Come for me," he says, his voice primal and raspy.

I realize he's panting just as hard as I am.

I moan as he thrusts again, bringing me so close.

"Come for me, princess," he says again.

This time, I do. I feel the warm waves of pleasure flow through me as I scream his name.

He comes right after me before collapsing on top of me. Our bodies stay pressed together for several minutes. In these few precious moments, our bodies are one.

And I know now that he will hurt me. As soon as he gets up and goes to clean himself off, he will rip me apart, taking a small part of me with him I can never get back. Because that was the best sex of my life. That's how sex is supposed to be. I just hope when he does finally leave, it only leaves a small hole in my heart instead of a gaping wound in his wake.

Heat creeps up my neck, waking me. I try to move, but I can't. Killian's body is heavy on top of mine. His stubble scratches against my chest when I try to move.

We fell asleep. I try to glance at a clock, but I don't find one. *How long have we been sleeping like this?* I try to move, and I find he is still buried inside me. Although he doesn't fill me quite the same way he did before.

This can't be happening. He was supposed to leave as soon as this was over. If anyone catches him leaving my room in the morning, we are going to be out of time to decide what we want to do. My grandfather will force us into getting married when that's clearly not what either of us wants. *So, why did Killian fall asleep on top of me then? If he doesn't want to be with me, why is he still here?*

"Killian," I whisper. I don't know why I'm whispering. Maybe it's because I'm ashamed of what we just did. I don't sleep with strange men—although Killian isn't a stranger anymore. I don't do this though. I'm a good girl. I don't sleep with someone on the first date—except I just did.

"Killian," I say louder.

He stirs slightly, but my voice isn't enough to wake him.

"Killian!" I say even louder.

His eyes open wide, and his body jerks off of mine. We both wince at the loss we feel as soon as his body leaves mine. I close my eyes and take a deep breath. I will not let the pain overtake rational thought. I will not.

"You need to go," I say without opening my eyes.

I feel his hand against my cheek, brushing my hair off my face. "If that's what you want," he says softly.

I keep my eyes closed, afraid I will cry if I open them. I refuse to be the woman who cries after sex. I will not let that happen. I will prove to him I can be just as heartless as him. I can sleep with a man without losing a bit of myself, without expecting more than one night.

"You need to go," I say again.

"Okay," he says.

I feel the bed shift as he stands from the bed. When I hear the bathroom door close, I open my eyes. I take another deep breath before getting up and walking to the closet. I slip on pajama pants and shirt. I grab a hair tie and quickly gather my hair in a bun on top of my head.

I glance at my phone. It's three in the morning. I sigh. I'm not going to get much sleep. I probably won't get any more sleep as soon as he leaves. But I need him gone before I do something stupid that will reveal I can't do this, just like he said I couldn't.

He comes back from the bathroom, but I don't glance at him as much as my body wants one last peek at his tight abs and impressive cock. I won't. I had my fun. Now, it's time to move on.

"I'll be in the living room," I say. I walk through the bedroom door and into the living room. I don't look back.

It only takes him a minute to get dressed. I glance up from my spot on the couch when he enters the living room. He's dressed. His hair is combed. He looks exactly like he did when he came to pick me up, completely unaffected by what just happened. He probably isn't affected. He does this once a quarter with different women all the time. I'm just his whore for the night.

Killian walks to me. He bends down and softly kisses me on the lips. "Sleep well, princess."

He walks to the door. I don't get up. I refuse to walk him to the door. That's what girlfriends do. That's what women in love do. I'm not in love, not even close.

My eyes follow him though. They follow him to the door. They watch as he pauses for just a second before he opens the door. His eyes meet mine. I swear they look sad, or maybe that's just my imagination. Probably just tired. I don't know. But then he opens the door, and he's gone.

I stay on the couch as one tear falls. It hurts, seeing him go.

Tonight was a mistake. I shouldn't have had sex with him...because I think I just fell a little for him. And if I fall for him, then that gives him the advantage. That means I will do whatever is in his best interest instead of what is in mine. I can't do that. I have to stay strong. I have to do what I need.

I should be angry with Killian. He lied to me. He took away another bit of my freedom. And I am. I am angry. I'm angry I didn't get to experience dating Eli for longer than I did. I'm angry I didn't date other men after Eli. I'm angry Killian is the only man who has ever made me feel loved... except it wasn't love. It was anger and passion. That's what made the sex so great. It wasn't real.

I wipe the fallen tear from my cheek, and then I grab the remote and turn on the TV. Tonight, for the first time, I don't think of my father and how much I miss him. Instead, I find a new hole in my heart, a hole that can only be filled by Killian. But it's a hole that will never be filled.

13

"Good afternoon, princess."

I freeze at the words. I was hoping I wouldn't see him today. Most of the executives don't work on the weekends. But, of course, that doesn't include Killian. Of course, he works on weekends. That's probably why he's so high up in the company at such a young age.

"What do you want?" I sound annoyed and angry. I'm both of those things right now. I didn't sleep a second after he left. I lift my coffee to my lips, trying to keep my aggravation and exhaustion at bay.

Killian raises his eyebrows. "Well, aren't you pleasant? Didn't sleep well?" He smirks.

My eyes shoot daggers in his direction, and he holds his hands up in defense, like I really was shooting something in his direction.

"What do you want?" I ask again, letting my anger I never got out last night bubble to the surface.

"I have a crisis I need your help with."

I roll my eyes and look back to the computer I finally

figured out the password to. It was *princess*. I should have known.

Killian walks to me. "I'm serious. You are the only one who can help with this. I even have your grandfather's approval."

That has my attention, although I don't know why Killian would suddenly be helping me. Maybe he feels guilty for tricking me into presenting in front of half of the company when he knew they would destroy me with their questions. Maybe he feels guilty for the breakup between the only boyfriend I ever had and me.

"What is it?"

"Come on, and I'll show you."

He reaches his hand out to me, but I don't take it. I stand and follow him out of my father's office. I follow him out to the pool at the back of the casino. That's when I realize what he wants.

"No," I say.

"Come on, Kinsley. Our other model got sick at the last minute. It's you, or we will have to pay thousands of dollars to have them come back to reshoot next week. It will also mean the ads will be delayed. We need you."

Damn it! I hate his pleading expression and puppy-dog eyes. I can't say no to him.

"Maybe," I say, sighing.

He smiles. "I'll take that as a yes."

I shake my head, but he takes my hand and leads me over to where people are standing around, doing nothing.

"Here's your new model," Killian says, thrusting me into the center of the group.

The man in charge smiles when he sees me. "You're Kinsley Felton. You've modeled for *Seventeen*."

I smile. "That's me."

The man's eyes light up. It feels good to be known for my modeling career and not because I'm Robert Felton's daughter.

"I'm Brock Parry. I'm in charge of the shoot."

I smile, shaking his hand.

"But wait...will you do this shoot for so little money?"

I raise my eyes. He has no idea who I am. It makes me laugh.

"I'm Robert Felton's daughter, the owner of the casino. Don't worry about paying me. I'm doing this to help the company."

Brock smiles with a small flush on his cheeks. "Sorry. Let's get you back to wardrobe."

I follow him, but I feel Killian's eyes on me the entire time as I walk back to a guest room serving as a makeshift wardrobe room. I just hope, when I come back out, he isn't still here because I'm not sure how I'll be able to do this job with him here.

———

I don't know why I didn't expect to be mostly naked in the ad. Maybe because this is a classy casino, but I guess I should have expected this. I should have expected I would be wearing a scantily clad bathing suit. My hair is teased and curled in large waves. I'm wearing more makeup than a hooker. I look sexy, I realize, as I stare back at myself in the mirror.

I've worn bathing suits in hundreds of ads before, but I never looked sexy. I looked cute and pretty. Right now though, I look hot. I take in a deep breath as I wrap my robe back around me. I'm going to have to channel my inner Scarlett to do this.

It's what I've always wanted—to be treated just like every other model, to be looked at as a woman instead of a girl. Here's my chance. I'm not going to blow it.

I strut out of the room and into the warm Las Vegas sun. We are shooting in front of the new pool that will be opening next weekend, but despite the pool being closed, there are hundreds of people gathered around, giving their two cents on the direction of the shoot.

I find Brock and am disappointed when I see Killian standing next to him. Brock smiles when he sees me. He hugs me, like he has known me my whole life. I try my best to embrace him back.

"You look fantastic," Brock says.

I smile. "Thanks."

"So, Killian was telling me the look we are going for in the ad. We want sexy, hot, spicy. We want people to want to come to our hotel because they think it's swimming with people as hot as you."

I glance back at Killian, who is smiling brightly. I roll my eyes. He's enjoying this.

"I got it," I say.

"Great. We will start with some dry shots of you posing on the lounge chair, and then we will get you in the water for the film portion."

I nod. It doesn't sound too hard. I walk over to where the camera is set up, remove my robe, and hand it to one of the assistants who helped me pick out the red bikini. I feel everyone's eyes on me. It would make most people nervous or shy—having this many eyes on them all at once, staring at their body. But I don't feel like that. I like how my body looks.

I lie back on the lounge chair and put my arms above my head. My first reaction is to smile. And then I remember this isn't a *Seventeen* magazine shoot. I'm supposed to look like sex. I drop my smile as I arch my back while looking at the camera. The camera clicks, capturing the look.

"Great, Kinsley. Arch your back just a little more, and drop your eyes," Brock says.

I do.

"Perfect."

I let my hand fall to my neck as I've seen Scarlett do hundreds of times before. More clicks.

"Yes. Just like that!" he shouts.

I stifle a laugh. It's funny how much it sounds like we are shooting a porno sometimes.

I see Killian standing just behind the camera. His smile is gone, but his intense stare never leaves my body. So, I increase the seduction, wanting him to miss my body as much as I miss his. I want him to regret hurting me.

My hand falls lower until it grazes my breast.

"Keep it right there."

More clicks.

When Brock gets the shot, I let my hand slowly drop lower down my stomach until it's just grazing the inside of my thigh.

Killian bites his lip in response.

More clicks.

"Now, move to your stomach."

I do. More clicks.

"We got it!" he shouts.

I smile and stand. I'm immediately handed my robe that I wrap back around my body.

"That was perfect," Brock says.

He hands me a small index card with a couple of lines on it. That's when I realize the video ad will not be solo. I'll be shooting it with a man. I smile inside. It will give me a chance to see how affected Killian is.

"We will have you get in the water and get your hair wet. Your makeup is waterproof, so you should be fine there, but if we need to do any touch-ups, we will do it then. Then, we will have Cedric jump in and swim up to you. That will be the first shot, and then we will proceed with the rest of the scene after that. We will have cue cards with your lines on it if you forget. Any questions?"

I glance down at my index card one more time, but I already have the simple lines memorized. "Nope, I got it."

I walk over to the pool and hand Brock my robe before diving into the cool water. I shiver as the cool water prickles my skin, despite the warm weather. When I come up for air, I remember the pool was just filled yesterday. It hasn't had time to warm up. I flip my hair back, knowing that's how they will want it for the shoot. I feel Killian's eyes burning into me as I do, and I smile. He's definitely affected. Now, let's see how affected. I swim over to the shallow end where they want me so they can see my body from the waist up.

I glance down to the other end of the pool and see Cedric standing at the edge. I smile. He's tall, muscular, and tan. I definitely won't mind doing the shoot with him. I glance over and smirk at Killian's reaction. His deep frown is clear from across the pool. He either didn't know Cedric was going to be a part of the shoot, or he forgot. Either way, he doesn't look happy.

"Action!" Brock yells.

Cedric dives into the pool. I keep my eyes on him as he swims up to me. He grabs me by the waist, and I smile and giggle as his hands make his way up my body as he surfaces.

"Cut. That was great. We will move on as soon as we adjust the camera."

"I'm Cedric," the man says, running his hand through his long dark locks.

"I'm Kinsley."

"I think I'm going to enjoy this," he says.

I smile. "Me, too."

Brock walks over to us. "All right, now, we want you two to make out until we call cut. We will probably do it several times here, and then we will move to under the waterfall."

We both nod. Cedric puts his hands around my waist. I do the same to him. We both know better than to move our hands to each other's faces. It would ruin the shot.

"Action," Brock says.

I close my eyes as Cedric's lips touch mine. He doesn't tentatively kiss me, like he is just getting to know me. He kisses me hard and fast, like he has done this hundreds of times before. I kiss him back with the same intensity.

He's a good kisser, I think.

He tugs on my bottom lip, and I can't help it as a low moan escapes my lips. He smiles against me, tugging harder, moving our bodies closer together.

One of my hands travels up to the base of his neck, deepening the kiss. His hips press harder against mine until I feel his erection.

"Yes, just like that," I faintly hear Brock shout to us.

But I'm too lost in the kiss to hear Brock. Cedric kisses me harder until my tongue is sizzling.

"Cut!" Killian shouts.

That's when Cedric and I stop. Our breathing is heavy as I tremble slightly, but I don't move out from Cedric's arms.

He is smiling at me. "That was amazing."

I nod, unable to speak. When I glance back at the camera, ready for the next direction, I see Killian's face. His nostrils are flared, and his eyes are protruding out of me imploring me to stop as he bares his teeth at Cedric. He's pissed. I smile and wave at him before diving under the water and moving over to the waterfall. He's definitely affected by me and jealous as hell.

Cedric swims up behind me.

"So, how long have you been modeling?" I ask as we wait for them to move the camera to get the new angle.

"Two years. You?"

"Since I was twelve."

He smiles. "I could tell you were more experienced than most women I've modeled with."

I smile although no one has ever called me experienced. I'm the furthest from it. Sure, I've done hundreds of shoots, but only a few have ever been make-out scenes. Most have been just fun, cute poses.

"Action!" Brock shouts.

We both move under the waterfall. I don't know why people think this is sexy because it isn't. It's the furthest thing from it. I laugh as Cedric moves up closer together until we are kissing again. This time, there is nothing sexy about the kisses. As we kiss, we are both struggling for air beneath the water drowning us.

"Cut," Brock calls quickly.

We immediately move apart. We both cough up the water that was drowning us earlier.

"We are going to move back to the lounge chair," Brock says.

We swim to the edge and hop out. I'm still coughing up water as I do. I feel a towel being wrapped around me, and I glance between coughs to thank the person when I see whose arms are wrapped around me. It's Killian.

"Are you okay?" he asks.

Another cough of water spews out. "Yes, just swallowed some water on that last shot. It's nothing I've haven't experienced before."

"You don't need to do this."

I smile at him. "Yes, I do."

"I'm not talking about the shoot. You don't have to make out with some guy to get back at me for something that happened three years ago," he says seriously.

"I'm not. This is what you wanted." My voice drops. "You wanted me to fuck you and then forget about you. That's what I'm doing."

I walk away from Killian and do my best to dry myself off before I find Brock standing next to the lounge chair I was on before.

"Kinsley, I want you lying on your back on the chair, like you were before. Cedric, I want you lying on top of her. I want you to kiss and then stroke her hair. Then, I want you both to deliver your lines to the camera."

I smile, but inside, I'm terrified. I hate this kind of shoot. This is where it gets intimate, especially since we are both still drenched. I will be able to feel every inch of Cedric's body as he lies on top of me...just like I felt every inch of Killian's body last night.

I lie down on the lounger, and Cedric smiles as he lies on top of me.

"Well, this is awkward," he says when his wet body forms with mine.

"Don't act like you aren't enjoying it," I say, trying to sound relaxed.

He smiles. "You're right."

I feel his hard chest and abs pushing against me. I feel his hot breath on my neck, his erection throbbing against my core.

My heart is beating fast as Brock has us look intimately into each other's eyes. His are blue and bright, not dark and intense like I'm used to staring into. Cedric is a good-looking guy, but he's not Killian.

"You're beautiful," Cedric whispers into my ear.

My cheeks flush. I take a deep breath, but it's hard to get any air with Cedric's body pressed against mine. I feel everyone's eyes on us as Cedric tucks a strand of hair behind my ear. I'm too frozen to move or react. I have to get my act together, so I don't come off looking like a bored mannequin instead of a sexy model flirting with Cedric, like I'm supposed to be doing.

I smile at him. "You're pretty handsome yourself," I whisper in his ear.

I feel his erection harden beneath me.

"I'm more than just a model, you know. I just graduated from UNLV with a business degree. I'm planning on going to law school this fall. This is just a way to pay the bills."

I don't know why he is saying this, but he seems genuinely proud of what he has accomplished. It's no Harvard, but I am impressed.

"That's impressive," I say.

Cedric's eyes look lustful now as they drop to my chest and then come back to my eyes. "I don't usually do this. I don't usually ask models I work with out on dates. I don't like mixing business and pleasure. But you're not one of the typical models I work with, and I can't help myself. Will you go out with me?"

My eyes grow wide. I've never been asked out by another model. It's the cardinal rule you never break. I glance over behind the camera to see what Killian is doing. My heart still has hope we can work things out together. I'm still holding out a small bit of hope last night was more than a one-night stand. His body language earlier made it seem like he was jealous, but I'm not sure if jealousy is enough for him to want anything more to do with me.

When I spot him, I see him talking to the spunky makeup artist. He's laughing. She's flirting. He's flirting back. I'm nothing to him but a problem he needs to get rid of.

I turn my attention back to Cedric. He's handsome. He seems nice. He even has a future planned out beyond modeling. And I need to get over Killian.

Who knows? If this turns into something, Granddad might think I am capable of finding my own husband.

"Sure. I'm free tonight," I say.

Cedric's smile and erection grow in unison. His body presses closer to mine. "Tonight is perfect."

He lowers his lips to mine, which surprises me because Brock never told us to kiss. This kiss is real. It's not planned. It's tentative and gentle, just testing the waters in a way most first kisses do. When I kiss him back, wrapping my arms around his neck, I try to keep myself from comparing this kiss to Killian's. Cedric deepens the kiss. His tongue easily slides into my mouth, like he has practiced this many times before. I don't care though. I feel his hand slide up and cup my breast, and I moan.

Shit, I moaned. I'm on camera, moaning, as a man I just met is feeling me up.

"Cut!" Killian shouts.

I look up and am shocked that he was the one yelling cut. He glares in our direction, but I don't know why. He walks over to us, as his face reddens and his jaw tenses.

His eyes travel to Cedric's and then mine. "This isn't a porno. Just kiss her, and then deliver your lines."

I gulp nervously as Cedric's body stays plastered to mine, but Cedric seems unaffected.

"Sorry, boss." Cedric looks back to me, winking as he does. "It's just hard not to get lost in a beautiful woman. I forgot I was doing a job."

"If you don't just do your job, you won't be getting paid, Cedric," Killian says.

Now, I'm glaring at Killian. That's taking it a little too far.

"Sorry. It won't happen again—at least, not until tonight," Cedric says, winking at me.

I giggle at Cedric. It wasn't the suavest of lines I've ever heard, but I don't care. I'm having fun, flirting with Cedric. I'm excited to see where he takes me to dinner tonight. That's two dates in two nights. I'm sure at this rate I can find a man my grandfather likes more than Killian. It was my father who was in love with Killian after all, not my grandfather. It might not be Cedric, but if I spend the next month dating, I'm sure I can do better.

I smile, happy to have a new plan. It's my own plan for my life. The modeling is fun, but it's not what I want my life to be.

"What does that mean?" Killian says.

"Kinsley agreed to go out with me tonight," Cedric says.

"Is that true?" Killian asks, looking at me.

My smile drops when I see a hint of sadness in his eyes. I don't know why he's sad. This is what he wanted—for me to live my own life.

"Yes," I say weakly.

Killian shakes his head. "Just finish the shoot. I'm not paying for overtime."

I watch as Killian walks away, but this time, he doesn't

stop. He walks back into the hotel. He doesn't finish watching the shoot. And I have no idea why he reacted like a complete ass.

I turn my attention back to Cedric, back to the job at hand. And I do my best to erase any thoughts of Killian from my brain.

14

———

I HEAR the knock on my door. I glance down at the time on my phone—seven fifty-five. He's five minutes early. I finish applying my red lipstick before I head to the door. I check through the peephole first before I open the door. Cedric is standing there in a suit. I exhale, happy I wore appropriate clothing for once.

I am happy with the response he gives me. His eyes drop to the cutouts on each side of the black dress before dropping lower to take in my exposed legs. When his eyes find mine again, I see the appreciation there.

"You look even more beautiful, if that's possible."

"It's possible. You look beautiful yourself," I say, eyeing his tailored suit and toned chest peeking out from atop his slightly unbuttoned shirt. "I mean, you look handsome," I say, flushing a bright shade of pink already.

"Don't be."

He holds his arm out for me, and I take it.

We walk down the hallway and into the elevator in relative silence. It's when we get to the casino floor I realize Cedric doesn't know that I'm Kinsley Felton, daughter of

143

Robert Felton. Maybe he won't notice the stares as we walk through the casino floor, arm in arm.

"Good evening, Kinsley," one of the bartenders says.

I nod my head in her direction, smiling. I try walking faster to get us out of here as soon as possible, but Cedric doesn't take the hint. Instead, he seems uneasy, as more and more employees begin staring at us. Some seem shocked to see me walking, hand in hand, with a man. Others smile knowingly. And others give me a friendly nod of recognition as we walk through the floor.

My nerves intensify when I see Killian sitting at the bar in the center of the casino floor. He's not alone; a dark haired young woman is sitting with him. She touches his arm and smiles. He grins back at her. I thought I was the only one he smiled at. I thought I was special. I'm not.

I tear my eyes from them as Cedric escorts me out the doors.

"Do you work here?" Cedric asks when we are outside.

"You could say that."

He stops us, as my answer didn't cure his curiosity.

"My name is Kinsley Felton. My father used to own the company. Everybody in there knows who I am because of it."

I run my hands through my long blond locks. I twist and twirl them as I wait for him to change how he acts around me, but he doesn't.

"That's cool." He shrugs. He begins walking again, but then he suddenly stops.

I curiously look at him. "Something wrong?"

"Wait...you don't work as one of the bartenders or something? I'm not sure I could handle dating someone who has men ogling them every night."

I laugh. "No, I'm not a bartender, but I am a model.

What do you think men do when they see my ads or magazine covers?" I raise an eyebrow at him.

"Good point." He sighs before he softly kisses me on the lips. It's a sweet kiss. It doesn't send fireworks exploding throughout my body though.

He pulls away with a look of contentment on his face. "I guess I'll just have to be jealous then."

I smile against his lips. "I guess so."

"I do like jealous sex."

I twist away from him. "Me, too," I say. But I've never had jealous sex before, and even though we spent half the day making out while mostly naked, I'm not sure I'm ready to have sex with Cedric.

He quickly catches up to me and loops his arm back around me.

"Where are we going?" I ask.

We walk less than a block when Cedric stops. "Right here."

I smile without looking at the restaurant we are stopped in front of. I already know which one it is. It's one of my favorites. My father has taken me here hundreds of times.

"Is this okay?" he asks.

"It's perfect."

We take a seat in the beautiful restaurant. A piano player plays softly in the background, and red roses sit in the center of the table.

"Do you like red wine?" Cedric asks.

"Yes," I say.

I glance down at the wine list and find that my favorite is listed, the one Killian got me hooked on. I'm just about to suggest it, but Cedric interrupts me.

"I think we should share a bottle of the house cabernet. Is that okay with you?"

I sigh. I'm not going to get my favorite. But that's okay; I don't want to be thinking about Killian anyway. And drinking that wine will make me think of him. It will make me wonder if he has already convinced the woman he was with to go to his room with him—although I don't think Killian would have to do much convincing. I think most women he meets would willingly jump into bed with him. That means, if he's asked, she's already made her way to his bed.

"Sounds perfect," I say, trying not to think about Killian.

I watch Cedric order our wine. It felt nice that he asked my opinion before just ordering for me. I'm so used to Killian, who orders whatever he wants for us both.

"Where did you go to school?" Cedric asks.

"Yale."

His eyes widen. "Seriously?"

My smile drops from my face. "Yeah, I studied theater... although I don't think that's what I want to do. I don't technically have my degree yet, but they should be sending it soon. I missed finals, but my grades were high enough I didn't need to make them up."

"Why did you miss finals?"

I look down, not ready to hear his *I'm sorry* that is going to follow what I say next. "My father died the weekend before finals."

He reaches his hand across the table and grabs ahold of my hand in a comforting manner. "I'm sorry."

I smile weakly. "Thanks."

An awkward pause passes where I don't want to talk further about my father, but Cedric isn't sure if he can change the topic or not.

"I'm not really sure about what I want to do next with my life," I say. That's not completely true though. I don't know *exactly* what I want to do with my life. I know it doesn't involve marrying Killian. I know it doesn't involve modeling. "What do you want to do once you finish your law degree?"

"I want to start my own firm. I like corporate law. And then I want to settle down with a beautiful girl like you. Somewhere warm."

"Of course," I say, smiling.

"And I want to marry her. I want to have kids with her. I want my life to be her."

I blush. "I hope you find that someday."

His eyes stay transfixed on mine. "I'm getting close."

His eyes sparkle, and I quickly lose myself in them. It would be nice to be married to someone like Cedric. He seems nice. He seems like a gentleman. He seems like husband material, unlike Killian who is too focused on his work to ever give proper attention to a wife and family.

"Kinsley?" my grandfather says.

I turn and see my grandfather standing at the end of our table. He has a stern look on his face. I see Killian standing behind him with a small smirk.

I try to pull my hand away from Cedric's, but he doesn't understand what's happening. He just tightens his grip as his thumb slowly moves over my palm.

"Hi, Granddad," I say.

"Who is this?" he asks, looking at Cedric.

"This is—" I start.

But, of course, Cedric, being a gentleman, jumps in immediately.

"I'm Cedric Allum. I'm her date for the evening—and, hopefully, if she will have me, for many dates after this."

I wince at his words, and Cedric looks at me in confusion.

"I'm not just a model," Cedric says in a rush, thinking that is the reason that my grandfather and I are so unhappy with what he just said. "I just do that on the side for some extra money, same as Kinsley. I just graduated with a business degree from UNLV. I got accepted into a law school in Chicago. I plan on being a lawyer, sir."

My grandfather is paying him no attention. Instead, he is looking at me. "I think you'd better end the date now, Kinsley."

I nod, unable to argue with him in such a public space. I don't look at Killian. And I don't look at Cedric as I begin to stand from my chair.

I take a deep breath before I do my best to look strong as I look at Cedric. "I'm sorry. You've been wonderful, but I think it's best if we stop this here."

"Why? I thought this was going well." He glances up at my grandfather. "If your grandfather and"—he looks at Killian—"your brother would like to join us, they are more than welcome. Then, they can get to know me a little better and feel more comfortable with us going out."

I chance a glance at Killian when Cedric calls him my brother. His smirk is gone. He's rubbing the back of his neck in annoyance instead of the fuming anger I was expecting. It seems he doesn't even see Cedric as worthy of a challenge.

"That won't be possible," Granddad says.

"Another time, then?" Cedric asks.

I smile weakly at his persistence, but he needs to learn when to give up.

That's when Killian steps forward. "I'm sorry, Cedric, but you need to go home and forget about Kinsley. Don't call her. Don't think about her. Don't try to reach out to her in any way. Plenty of other girls are out there who would be more suited to you."

I close my eyes to keep the sting out of them after what he just said.

"I think Kinsley is plenty suited to me," Cedric says.

"No, because Kinsley is *my* fiancée," Killian says.

Cedric gasps. Then, he looks to my left hand to find a ring that isn't there. His eyes narrow in my direction. "You're engaged?"

I twist my hair as I look at him. I don't know how to answer that. I'm not technically engaged. At least, I wasn't the last time I spoke with either of the men glowering over me, but it's too complicated to say I'm not engaged.

Cedric takes my lack of an answer as an answer. "She's all yours," he says as he throws his napkin down on the table before storming out.

I don't bother to follow him with my eyes when he leaves. I feel like crying. I feel like going home and spending the night taking a long warm bath, trying to forget what just happened. I feel like screaming at Killian and Granddad for what they just did.

"Come on, Kinsley. We have a table for us set up upstairs. We will have them add another chair. You'll eat with us," Granddad says. His voice is dripping with disappointment.

I nod, unable to say any words without losing it. I feel so embarrassed. I watch as my grandfather begins walking, but Killian hovers over me, waiting for me to follow my grandfather.

I take a second. "How could you?" A tear falls.

"You can't be with him. He's not a good guy."

"And you are?" I shake my head in frustration. "You can't tell me you want me to make my own decisions about my life and then make every decision for me! You can't tell him I'm your fiancée one minute but then tell me you don't want to marry me the next. You can't pick up a random stranger at a bar one minute and then say I can't go on a date myself. Talk about indecisive. What do you want, Killian? Other than the CEO position, what the fuck do you want?"

I close my eyes when I realize I just cursed in front of a table with children. I never curse. But Killian brings out the worst in me, the absolute worst.

"I want to marry you," are the words that leave his lips.

15

———

I HAVEN'T LOOKED at Killian since I sat down at the table opposite my grandfather. I can't. I don't believe what Killian said when we were alone downstairs. He didn't say anything else. It was just those five words.

"I want to marry you."

I don't believe them. I don't think I ever will until I see him down on bended knee. And even then, it won't be because that's what he really wants. It will be because that is the only way he can become CEO.

"What were you doing with that boy, Kinsley?" my grandfather asks.

Our waiter interrupts us, and my grandfather orders wine for the table. He asks Killian for his opinion but not mine.

When the waiter leaves, Granddad turns his attention back to me, waiting for my answer.

"He was nice. I met him at the modeling shoot earlier. I didn't realize I wasn't allowed to date while I waited for Killian to decide if he wants to marry me or not," I snark.

I feel Killian's eyes on me, but I still don't look at him.

I'm too pissed to look at him. He did the same thing an hour earlier with a woman. *Why can't I?*

"You know the rules, young lady. The same rules still apply as when your father was alive. If you want to date, you run the guys by me. I will tell you whom you should or shouldn't date. You've made too many horrible decisions in the past to allow anything else. You shouldn't have been on a date with Cedric."

"I've made one horrible mistake. One," I say, glaring at my grandfather for bringing it up.

My eyes dart to Killian, but his searching eyes shooting back and forth between the two of us make it clear he doesn't know what we're talking about.

I move on. "What was wrong with Cedric? He seemed like a perfect gentleman if you asked me."

"Tell her, Killian."

Killian takes a deep breath. "Cedric is a scam artist. He only dates rich women and then scams them or steals money from them."

I turn to him. "And how exactly do you know this?"

"We do background checks on all our employees, including the models. There were some suspicious things when his returned. The suspicious information didn't touch my desk until after the shoot. Otherwise, I would never have let him do the shoot. He's a wanted felon in three states. We called the police. He was arrested as soon as he left the premises."

Fuck! How the hell am I supposed to make my own decisions in my life when I keep making the wrong ones?

The waiter pours us each a glass of wine, and I down my glass in one gulp. I can feel everyone's eyes on me as I do, but I don't care. The waiter pours me a second glass.

"This is why you can't make your own decisions without

consulting Killian or me. You are too naïve, too easily taken advantage of, sweetheart. We are just trying to protect you."

I don't respond to Granddad's words, but I can't believe them. I didn't do anything, except go on a date with Cedric. I didn't make up my mind about him yet. If they had just given me time, they could have seen I would have turned Cedric down on my own.

"Are you ready to order?" the waiter asks.

My grandfather nods. "I'll have the sirloin, medium rare. Kinsley will have the same."

I don't hear Killian order. I'm too busy sulking. This is what my life will be like. Everything will always be decided by these two men. I will never get a choice in what I eat or drink. I will never get a choice in what I do. I will never get a choice in when I have children or what their names will be or what they do with their own lives. I will never get a say. I've never had a say.

I quickly sip on my wine, and before I know it, I've finished another glass. The waiter immediately fills it again.

"Regardless, I have some good news to share with you, Kinsley," Granddad says.

I'm not hearing him though. My head is spinning. I'm dizzy. I've felt this way once before, and I know what's going to happen next. I can't be here when it happens.

"Excuse me. I think I'm going to be sick," I say as I stand from the table.

I rush to find the restroom down on the first floor. I run, barely making it to a toilet stall before the contents from my stomach come back up.

God, I hate alcohol, I think as I heave into the disgusting public toilet.

A few seconds pass, and I hear the door swing open. *Great.*

Now, whoever has walked through that door will get to hear my embarrassment as I puke into the toilet.

I try to reach back to at least lock the stall door to keep the woman from seeing me, but I can't without moving away from the toilet, and my stomach isn't finished emptying yet.

That's when I feel his arms on me. Killian's holding back my hair as he slowly rubs my back.

"It's okay, princess."

I want to fight Killian off, but I'm too weak to do that. I vomit again and again, to my disgust. I can't believe he is in here, taking care of me like a real boyfriend would. But we aren't boyfriend and girlfriend. We aren't even friends. We are nothing.

When I finally finish, I feel like collapsing, but Killian holds me up.

"Come on, princess. Let's get you cleaned up."

Killian helps me stand and leads me to the sink. I watch as he turns on the warm water and puts a paper towel under the water before wiping my face.

He doesn't say anything. He just intently stares at me. There isn't disappointment on his face. There is just nothing. It's like he is doing a business transaction. That's what I am. I don't have to be stupid to know what my grandfather was about to say. He was going to tell me that Killian agreed to marry me. I'm not ready to hear those words from him. If he says them and I hear them, then it's over. I have nothing left to fight for. My destiny has already been decided, but I'm not ready to know what my future entails yet.

"I want to go home," I say.

He nods. "I sent your grandfather home. I told him I'd make sure you got home okay. I told him you would talk to him tomorrow."

"Thanks," I whisper.

I follow Killian out of the restroom. A woman, who was just about to enter, stares wildly at Killian. She's probably thinking we just hooked up in the restroom. I see Killian smirk at her, and my cheeks blush.

I make it out of the restaurant without stumbling, but Killian scoops me up.

"I can walk," I protest while hating and loving being in his arms. I hate the conflicting feelings.

"I know, princess, but you shouldn't have to."

I don't fight him. I just let him carry me into the casino. I let him carry me, despite the stares we get on the casino floor. I don't care. Let them think what they want about me. My life is over anyway.

To my surprise though, Killian doesn't take me to my room. He takes me to his. I don't protest. I'm too tired to do anything else. And we have some shit we need to work out anyway.

He lays me on his bed that is just like the one in mine. He leaves and quickly comes back with some water, aspirin, and the hotel's cookies. He hands them all to me. He doesn't have to speak to get me to take them. I know they will make me feel better.

"You shouldn't drink so much."

"No shit," I say before swallowing the pills.

He smiles. "You're cute when you curse."

"I learned from you." I sigh. "What do you want, Killian? Why am I here?"

He narrows his eyes at me. "Why did you agree to go out with him?"

I sigh. "Why not? I know what happened between us last night was just a one-time thing. And I just thought, if I could prove I am capable of finding a man on my own, one who is good for the company and good for me, then my grandfather would give me more time to be more involved in the decision. I just thought I could do better than you."

I study his face to see if my words hurt him, but they don't. "And you were out with that brunette at the bar anyway."

A small smile tugs at the corner of his lips. "That was my sister."

"Oh." I take a deep breath. "Why did you agree to marry me?"

"Because I want to be CEO. And I've realized this is the only way I will ever get what I want."

I sit up too fast, and the dizziness that ensues makes me grab my head. He grabs ahold of me and forces me to lie back in bed.

"I just want to go back to my own bed."

"No, not until we figure this out."

I sigh. "There is nothing to figure out. You want to marry me to get the CEO position, but you don't really want to be married to me. I don't want to marry you either. I'll tell my grandfather I don't care about the money or being connected to the Felton empire. You'll get everything you ever wanted."

"That won't work."

"It will. It was your plan after all. And you do no wrong, remember?"

"That's not true." His body moves closer to mine. "I do a lot of things wrong. I do a lot of things I shouldn't do."

I roll my eyes. "You've never done anything wrong in your life."

His lips crash with mine, burning into me full of hunger, of need. I feel my body giving in to the kiss, but I can't let it happen.

I push him away. "What was that?"

"It was me doing something I shouldn't."

"Why shouldn't you?"

"Because you can't fall for me," he says.

But when he kisses me again, I wonder if he is the one who can't fall for me.

I push him off of me. But his mouth finds my neck instead of my lips.

"I'm still mad at you," I say.

His mouth tugs at my earlobe. "I know."

"I'm still mad at you for making Eli break up with me."

I moan when he nips at the lobe.

"I know."

"I'm still mad at you for ruining my date with Cedric."

He tangles his hand in my hair, tugging my head back, so his lips have better access to my neck. "I know."

"I'm still mad—"

"I know." He moves his mouth back to my lips, shutting me up.

I'm about to make a terrible choice. As his tongue caresses mine, I know I'm going to end up fucking him again. His hands slide down the sides of my body, feeling my curves.

"Fuck, I want you, princess." His greedy eyes take in my body, but it's not good enough to see me in the sexy dress. He wants more.

His mouth kisses down my neck to the edge of the dress. His hands grab at the top, and when I don't protest, he rips the dress in half. It's the sexiest fucking thing I've ever seen.

His eyes now lust with a need to have my body. His hand grabs my breast without him asking, without him waiting to see if this is what I want. I've already told him with my parted lips, with my lust-filled eyes, with my heavy breathing. They all tell him how badly I want him, too.

"This is wrong," I say.

He takes my exposed nipple in his mouth. He twirls his tongue around the hard bud, making me forget why this is wrong as I moan his name. He grabs my other breast and twirls his thumb around it.

"Maybe," he says.

It makes me smile at him. He smiles back before disappearing between my legs. He pulls my panties down with his teeth, leaving me completely naked while he is still fully clothed. I grab at his shirt, and he gets the hint. He rips his shirt off. I watch as a few buttons fall to the sides. He stands and unzips his pants, removing them and his underwear.

He moves back on top of me, his lips hovering above mine. "I can't believe you let him kiss this," he says, running his thumb across my lips before devouring them with his own. "These lips are mine, not his." He kisses me again harder, marking me as his own, showing me how jealous he really was when I was kissing Cedric. "He doesn't have a right to these lips."

He bites on my bottom lip, tugging on it like Cedric did earlier, but when Killian does it, liquid pools between my legs.

When he releases it, I repeat his words, "These lips are yours."

He smiles at me. He moves down my chest and finds my breasts. He roughly grabs them, rougher than he has before. He takes one in his mouth, nipping hard at the nipple.

"He doesn't get to see these nipples. He doesn't get to taste their hard peaks or hear you moan his name as he drives you crazy."

I moan as his tongue drives me wild. "Just yours."

He moves lower, stopping between my legs. He takes my clit into his mouth, sucking ferociously, making it his. "He doesn't get the pleasure of watching you come."

I moan, "No, only you."

When he's done, he leans back and flips me over onto my stomach. He smacks my ass, hard. It stings, but it somehow also brings me pleasure.

"This ass? It's mine, not his."

"I'm yours, all yours," I moan.

He smacks me again before he pulls me onto all fours. I hear him rustle with the wrapper of a condom before I feel him pushing at my entrance.

"You remember that, princess, before you go on another date. You remember that, when you get back, I'm going to punish you like I'm going to punish you now. You don't deserve to come. You don't deserve to feel good. You deserve to be punished for not understanding that you're mine."

He thrusts inside me without warning. It hurts at first as he fills me. This time, instead of going slow, he moves fast, but this time, I accommodate him. It feels good, going faster.

"Fuck, Killian," I moan.

He slaps my ass again, and I cry out.

"Do you understand how jealous you made me?" He slaps me again as he thrusts inside.

"Yes," I moan.

"Will you do it again?" He crashes into me again.

"No, never," I moan as his balls crash into my clit.

"Why?"

He thrusts again, bringing me close, so close.

"Because I'm yours," I pant.

His hand reaches around, massaging my clit, as he crashes his body into me again.

"You can come, princess," he says as he massages my clit.

And I do. My body convulses as the waves wash through me. Killian follows right after, and we both collapse into a pile on the bed. His breath feels hot on my neck.

"You're mine, princess," he says before kissing me on the neck. "Your body, your soul, your mind, all mine."

Then, he gets off me to go clean himself off in the bathroom, leaving me spent on his bed.

A large smile is stuck on my face. Cedric was right. Jealous fucking is definitely the best.

I don't know what this means. *Does Killian like me more than he has been letting on?* I can feel my heart already falling for him. It's not just because the sex was the best thing I've ever felt. It's because he took care of me in a way no one ever has. He knew what I needed. He knew I needed him to feel jealous. He knew I needed him to own me. He knew I needed him.

———

I feel my time running out as I slip out of Killian's bed. He's still sound asleep, snoring, facedown on the bed.

Last night was amazing. By far, it was the best time I've ever had with a man. But it was just his way of trying to control me. He was manipulating me to do what he wanted. He doesn't care about me. And he sure doesn't love me.

I shake my head at myself. I can't believe he got me back in his damn bed. I used to be able to tell men no so easily. That woman is gone. At least around Killian.

I find my ripped dress on the floor. I can't put it back on. I go into the closet and find a T-shirt I doubt he will miss and slip it on over my head. I also find a pair of his workout shorts and slip those on. If anybody sees me, they will know for sure what happened last night, but it doesn't matter anymore. My time is running out.

I collect my ripped dress and purse off the floor.

Killian snores loudly, making me pause at his bedroom door to look at him. My heart aches as I look at him lying in bed. If I stayed for just a few more hours, I'm sure we would spend the morning together fucking and eating breakfast. It's what I want—to spend more time with Killian. But every moment I spend with him, the further I fall under his spell. I become more attracted to the idea of marrying him, of letting him run my father's company.

I can imagine it now. It would be a life of fucking, a life of butting heads, a life of me giving up my control. Our life together would be intense. I might even be able to love this man and have kids with this man.

The only problem is, he would never feel the same way about me. He would always resent the fact he was forced to marry me to get the job of his dreams. He would resent being forced to give up his life of banging different girls to come home to the same boring woman every night. He would resent his stolen life.

I can't do that to him. I can't do that to me. I don't know how to avoid that outcome without a fight though. And it's a fight I'm not sure I can win. But I have to try.

As much as I want to stay here and be kissed awake by this man, I can't, so I do the only thing I can do. I leave without a word, without a good-bye, without any explanation.

I make it back to my hotel room without anyone seeing me. It is four in the morning, so I wasn't expecting too many people to be roaming the halls, but this is Las Vegas. Anything and everything happens here.

I close the door to my hotel room and lean against it, taking a deep breath. I can't be around Killian anymore. I'll destroy both of our lives if I am.

I take the neck of the T-shirt I'm wearing and bring it up to cover my nose before taking a deep breath. I relax when I realize it smells like him. I take several more deep breaths before I make my way to my bed. I leave his shirt on and climb under the covers. I set my alarm for two hours from now. I drift back to sleep as I breathe in his manly scent, imagining his arms are wrapped around me instead of the shirt. The only decision I know is I'm done giving up control over my own life.

16

———

I KNOCK on Tony's office door a few hours before I'm supposed to meet my grandfather. I need to spend some time at the company—figuring out what life would be like here, what it would be like to run or even be a part of this company. Maybe then I might realize that this isn't really what I want. That would make it easier to walk away.

"Come in," Tony says from his desk.

I push the door open and sigh when I see the mess his office is in. If it's possible, I think it looks worse than it did the last time I was here. Now, there are empty plates of food rotting from what looks to be lunch from a previous day.

"Just wanted to see how you were doing," I say. But that's not true. I'm trying to figure out how I'm doing. I'm trying to figure out if I really belong here or if I'm just kidding myself.

"I'm doing all right. The real question is, how are you doing?"

I shrug as I walk into his office and take a seat across from him. "I've been better."

Tony gets up from behind his desk and takes a seat next to me. "Your father was one of the greatest men I ever knew.

He was kind. He was fair." He chuckles. "He was incredibly strong. He didn't take any crap from anyone." He looks at me. "You're a lot like him."

I shake my head. "I'm not as strong as him. I'm not strong enough to carry on his legacy. I can't even convince people to do a simple expansion that is obviously needed. I can't even decide what drink to order or what food to eat. I can't even choose the right men to date."

I look up to see Tony smiling at me.

"I never said your father was perfect—or that you are either, sweetie. I just said you were both strong."

"I wish my father had told me what I was supposed to do—if he really wanted me to do what my grandfather wanted or if he wanted something else."

Tony sighs. "Now, that is something I can't answer for you. What I think matters most is what you want, what you think you were born to do. Whether that's finding a way to run the company yourself, marry Killian, or run off and have nothing to do with the company, the decision is yours."

My eyes widen at his words. "How did you know about Killian or about me possibly wanting to run the company?"

His words are warm as he says, "Oh, honey, the whole company knows you are supposed to marry Killian. Your grandfather isn't the best at keeping secrets. And you? You're easy to read. I know the only reason you are spending any time with an old man like me is to try to learn, to see if this is the path for you."

"Then, you know it's not really my choice, my future. It's my grandfather's. It's Killian's. It's not mine."

Tony frowns. "That's where you are wrong. It's yours. Your father always made sure of that."

"What do you mean?"

"It's not my place to say."

A knock interrupts us.

"Hey, Tony." A young man sticks his head into Tony's office. "Have you seen Killian?"

Tony shakes his head. "No, sorry. I think he's at a meeting at the Felton Red Waves. He won't be back until later this evening."

"Shit," the man says. "Is Lee around?"

I glance down at my phone. "I don't think he is going to be in for another hour."

"Shit," the man says again. "I need someone to sign these, approving the initial demolition, and I need it now. They already showed up. If I don't give them these forms, like, right now, they are going to leave. Then, who knows when the construction will start?"

"I'll sign them," I say without thinking.

The man looks at me in confusion. "Who are you?"

"I'm Kinsley Felton. I'll sign them. It's no big deal really," I say, although I don't have authority to sign anything. Grandfather won't care though. I already know he wants the expansion to happen, and so does Killian. It won't hurt anything for my signature to be on it instead of theirs.

The man looks to Tony, who nods his head and smiles.

The man still looks concerned, but he knows his ass is on the line if the project doesn't start today. He rushes the papers over to me and shows me where to sign. I sign and initial each spot, barely glancing at the papers. I should probably read them before signing, but this man is in an obvious rush. I don't want to give him a heart attack by waiting for me to read them. And it feels good to be making a decision for the company even if it is one that has already been agreed upon.

"Thanks," the man says, rushing back out of Tony's office.

When I turn back to Tony, his sly smile is plastered on his lips.

"What?"

He shakes his head as he tries to lose the smile, but he can't. "I think, with a little training, you would make an excellent CEO. You probably shouldn't start off in that position, but I think a few years under your belt would get you ready."

"You're crazy. All I did was sign some papers. I didn't do anything."

"You did more than just sign some papers. You convinced a man who has never met you that you were in charge. And don't think I didn't notice that, after you left last time, you didn't just change one small thing about my numbers. You completely redid everything to make it work. You saw trends no one else saw. That's impressive. You are obviously a natural when it comes to numbers and finance. We could use someone like you in this department."

I smile weakly. "Thanks." But I don't feel like I'm capable of doing anything.

Tony stands, returning back to his chair. "Killian is good-looking and charming, too, though. He wouldn't be a terrible choice either." He winks at me. "There is no wrong choice, as long as you are the one making the choice. Be a housewife. Be a model. Become CEO. Decide what you want and go after it."

I frown. I don't want him giving me dating advice, although the other advice I appreciate. I don't want anyone giving me dating advice. He doesn't understand what's going on in Killian's head.

"He doesn't care about me. He just wants to marry me to get the position."

Tony narrows his eyes. "I wouldn't be too sure about

that. Word is, he just got promoted without marrying you. He might care more about you than you think."

But all I hear is that Killian got promoted to CEO. Last night, he knew the decision my grandfather had made. And Killian chose not to tell me my time was already up.

I no longer get a choice. At least not about becoming CEO.

"I need to go," I say.

Tony nods as I stand and leave without a goodbye.

<hr>

I take my phone out to call my grandfather, to tell him to meet me earlier, it can't wait. I dial his number, but I get his voicemail. I end the call before I leave a message. That's when I notice the messages from Killian.

There are three text messages, asking why I left this morning without talking to him, telling me we need to talk, telling me what to do.

I also notice the seven missed calls and two voicemails from him. I delete the voicemails without listening to them. I don't want to hear what Killian has to say. If he couldn't say it last night before fucking me, then I don't want to hear it now.

I pace back and forth thirty-five times in my father's office before I hear the familiar creak of the door being pushed open. My grandfather is standing in the doorway. He doesn't look happy to see me, but I don't give a shit.

I can't wait any longer, and the words fall from my mouth. "You made Killian CEO!" I shout at him.

He calmly walks in, setting a briefcase down on the desk. He doesn't say anything or even acknowledge me as he takes a seat behind my father's desk.

"You made Killian CEO," I say again, only slightly calmer.

He sighs in frustration. "Yes."

"I thought he had to marry me first. I thought it had to be agreed upon between the three of us."

"He did. He signed the papers yesterday afternoon, agreeing to marry you in six months. So, in good faith, I promoted him to CEO. He doesn't have the shares yet. That will happen after the wedding."

"What if I don't agree to the wedding?"

"You will. You don't have another choice. This is what is best for you."

"No, it's not. I don't want this. I don't want to be married to a man who doesn't love me. I don't want to marry someone just because you wished I were a grandson instead of your granddaughter. I won't do it."

"Kinsley, stop this. You will marry Killian. He's a good man. And I know he cares about you."

"You're wrong. He doesn't give a fuck about anything other than his work and finding his next good fuck."

His face turns red at my words. I take a deep breath, realizing what I just said to my grandfather. I've never cussed in front of him. I've never talked so crudely.

But, right now, he's not my grandfather. He's the enemy trying to control my life.

He calms his face before walking over to stand in front of me. He places both hands on either side of my shoulders. "This is what your father wanted, princess. He wanted you to marry Killian. He wanted you to support Killian in the role of running the company. He wanted you to have children to pass this company along to—just as my father did, just as I did to your father, just as your father is doing to you."

I feel a tear slip out of my eye. "But that's not what my father is doing. That's not what you are doing. I'm not getting the company with the same conditions as you got the company with or the same conditions as my father got. I'm being forced to marry someone, and only then do I get any say in the company. I'm not getting the same terms."

He smiles, like he thinks he's got me now, like he thinks he's won. "See? That's where you are wrong, Kinsley. You are getting the same terms as everyone else in the family. We all had marriages arranged by our parents. We all had marriages that were for the betterment of the company."

I frown as his words sink in. His words can't be true.

"That's not true. Mom and Dad met in college their junior year."

He shakes his head. "No, your mother was the daughter of the chairman of the Nevada Gaming Commission. We were having some trouble with getting our newest casino approved. Your father fixed the problem, proving his loyalty to the company and this family above everything else."

My mouth drops. I had no idea. I always thought my parents were in love. I always thought they cared about each other but maybe not. That might be why my father spent so many nights alone in his casinos instead of at home with my mother. That can't be true though. My mother was devastated when Dad died. She still is.

"You're lying."

He shakes his head. "Ask your mother."

I plan on it. "It doesn't change anything. I still won't marry Killian."

"You're stubborn, just like your father. He eventually caved though. You will, too." He glances at his watch. "You need to go home and get ready. I had a dress sent to your hotel room. I don't know why you stay here when you have a beautiful room at home." He sighs. "Be ready at eight tonight. That's when Killian will be picking you up."

I shake my head. "I'm not marrying him."

"Maybe not. But he at least deserves the respect of you telling him to his face."

I nod. "I'll go."

He's right. I need to put an end to whatever this is that's going on between Killian and me. I turn to leave, but his words stop me.

"There's one more thing you should know before you make a decision. If you refuse to marry Killian, the money is gone. I control the trust your father left you. You will have nothing but a theater degree to find you work. I'll call everyone and tell them never to hire you as a model again. You are doing this, or you are no longer my granddaughter. If you walk away from this, you are no longer a Felton."

Those are the words that will haunt me for the rest of the day. For the rest of my life.

"You are no longer a Felton."

I wish they were true. I wish I were never born a Felton.

I'd thought my future was entirely out of my control. I was wrong.

My grandfather just gave me control. I just don't like my choices.

17

———

I don't wear the cream-colored dress lying on my bed when I get back to my hotel room. It's a beautiful dress, one I'm sure my grandfather spared no expense to get for me. But I'm not wearing it. I don't know if it's because he chose it or if it's because it's an act of defiance to wear anything but that dress; possibly my last act of defiance. I don't know if it's because I can't stand to wear any color that resembles a wedding gown. I don't know if it's because I have a beautiful red dress I love and haven't had an occasion to wear it to. Whatever the reason, I chose red.

I stand in my hotel room in my deep red ballgown. I'm no closer to deciding if I'm going to say yes or no when Killian asks me. And I know he'll ask me. That's what tonight is about. That's why I'm wearing this pretty dress. That's why I've spent hours fixing my long blond hair. That's why I've spent hours covering my face in makeup.

Tonight is the night I decide the rest of my life. I just don't know what future that will be.

I hear the knock on the door. I glance at my phone. It's eight on the dot. Killian's on time tonight. I peek through

171

the hole in the door and see him dressed in a tux. I take a deep breath, and then I open the door.

I watch him lick his lips as his eyes travel over my body. I hold my breath, trying to calm my beating heart, but it doesn't slow. His eyes catch mine, and it's not a look of lust peering back at me although a hint of that is still there. It's a look I've never seen come from his eyes, and I have no idea what it means.

For a second, I imagine this is how it feels when you are in love, and you know tonight is the night—the night your life will change forever, the night he will get down on a nervous knee and ask you to marry him.

If only I could find someone who would do this for real...

If only he were doing this for more than a promotion...

If only I were doing this for more than family loyalty...

He regroups himself and puts a fake smile on his lips. "I wasn't sure you would answer."

I return his fake smile. "I wasn't sure you would come."

"You didn't return my calls."

"I deleted the voicemails."

He sighs. "We have a lot to talk about."

I nod, but I don't say anything. I give him no indication of how I feel, of how I will answer when he asks—not that I even know myself.

He sighs again. "Let's go, princess."

We walk out of the hotel and casino without saying a word. I don't say a word until we make it out onto the street where I see a horse and carriage waiting for us.

I gasp when I see it. I wasn't expecting anything like it.

"I thought you deserved the full princess experience."

I smile as he helps me into the carriage before climbing in next to me. I really do feel like a princess in this thing. I'm not sure if that's a good thing or a bad thing though. I'm not sure I like being a princess. A princess, I've realized, has no control over her life. Her life is to her country, to her family. It's just like how I live my life for the company, for my family.

I wasn't expecting this. I wasn't expecting effort from a man who was just doing this because he had to. I was expecting dinner and a proposal. But I'm afraid he's put more effort into it than that.

The carriage takes us down the main strip and then turns off, moving us throughout the city. I have no idea where we are going. I'm not sure I care. I'm lost in this perfect moment.

Killian places his arm around my shoulders, and I lean my head against his chest.

"I'm sorry," he whispers.

"For what?" I breathe back.

"For lying to you. For breaking you and Eli up. For controlling any bit of your life. For ruining your date. For forcing you into a life you don't want. For everything."

"None of this is your fault." I suck in a deep breath. "You don't have to do this though. You already have the job. It's not going to be taken away just because you don't do this."

I pause, waiting for him to confirm or deny my statement. He does neither. He just looks at me with the same intensity he always does.

So, I continue, "We don't even know each other. I don't know how many siblings you have. I don't know your parents' names. I don't know your favorite color or food or band. I don't know where you grew up. I don't know why you are such a workaholic. I don't know why you never want to get married or have kids. I don't know if we are compatible together. I don't know anything about you, other than you are good in bed and intelligent enough to run the company."

His expression grows grave, but he doesn't say a word.

"I'm a huge Justin Bieber fan—like, huge. I've seen him in concert six times. My favorite movie is *The Notebook*. I've watched it at least a hundred times, and I still cry every single time. I have enough clothes and makeup to fill three regular-size rooms. I hate large houses. I'd prefer to live in hotel rooms for the rest of my life.

"It is always going to take me longer than it should to make my mind up about what I want to order and even longer to make up my mind about anything else. And I'm only occasionally going to be okay with you making those decisions for me although you'll never really know when I want you to decide for me or when I want to make my own decisions.

"I'm never going to be okay with just being a housewife. I'm always going to want to find a way to fight my way into a leadership position at the company. I'm always going to want the fairy tale. I'll always want to be desperately in love and have kids," I say.

His hand reaches up to my lips, squeezing them together, silencing me. "It doesn't matter," he says, never taking his eyes off mine. He slowly releases my lips.

"It does. Trust me, you don't want to be stuck listening to Justin Bieber for the rest of your life when you prefer Justin Timberlake."

He chuckles. "I don't really like either."

"What? You don't like JT?"

"No," he says, like I'm crazy.

I shake my head. "See? You can't do this. Your life would be filled with the music of Justins and little kids running around and indecisiveness." I tuck my hair behind my ear.

"It's not what you want." But I'm not sure who I'm convincing with that statement.

As I stare into his eyes, I want to know everything about him. I want to listen to whatever crappy music he enjoys. I want to meet his parents and siblings. I want to argue with him about how long it takes me to order. I just don't want to marry him.

The carriage stops in front of Crystal Waterfalls, my favorite casino. My eyes are wide as I stare at him. He climbs out before holding his hand out to me. I take it, and he helps me out.

Killian doesn't let go of my hand as we walk into the building that, to my surprise, is empty. I don't see a soul walking around. I blink rapidly, thinking what I'm seeing is a dream. It's not. The casino is a ghost town.

I see a trail of rose petals on the floor. It starts next to the river that goes through the center of the hotel and casino. I let go of Killian's hand as I make my way over to the edge of the river. I let my hand dip into the cold water, like I have done hundreds of times before. Petals are floating on top of the water.

I slowly follow the trail of rose petals as I hear Killian walking behind me, but he doesn't try to walk next to me. He lets me discover everything by myself.

The rose petals follow the river. I follow them through the main casino floor, going past all the flashing lights of the slot machines, past the empty card tables, past the shops and restaurants. I follow them until they get to the door. It's the door to my favorite place in the world.

I hesitate at the door, trying to calm my beating heart. This is it. I push the door open, and at the same time, I suck in a breath.

It's beautiful, even more beautiful than usual. Lights are

strung over every tree. And the smell from all of the roses and fresh flowers in the garden overwhelm me, as they always do whenever I step into the hotel's garden. The waterfall rushes water over its crest just as calmly as it always does.

But what has taken my breath away are the rose petals and candles covering the floor. It looks like tiny shining stars on the floor of the garden.

I slowly turn back to the door. Killian is standing in the doorway, looking at me with a smile on his face. His head cocks slowly to the side as I smile back at him.

It's a fairy tale in here. It's just not real.

I feel my body tremble as he walks silently to me until he is standing just inches from my body. I hear music start up in the distance. I glance away from Killian and see a violinist playing. I turn back to Killian.

"I would have had her play Justin Bieber, if I had known."

His words make me smile a little brighter, but my body is still trembling.

I watch his tongue run over his lip. I want his tongue on my lip.

"My favorite movie is *The Hangover*. It makes me laugh every fucking time. I have a surprisingly little amount of clothing. I love playing poker and blackjack, even when I'm getting beaten by you. My parents both live in Las Vegas. I've lived here my entire life. I have one younger sister close to your age, one older sister, a brother-in-law—whom you already met—and a three-year-old nephew whom I would do anything for. I'm a workaholic. I'm stubborn. I'm controlling. I hate waiting for decisions. I've never wanted to get married. I've never wanted kids. I don't have a favorite artist, but I've been listening to the song 'Let Her Go' by Passenger on repeat lately."

I swallow hard. He's not going to propose. My head drops slightly in disappointment. This is good though. He needs to happy. At least one of us should be. I can give him that.

My eyes widen though when I watch him drop to one knee as he holds my hand.

"Princess, I know we might not know everything there is to know about each other. I know we, on paper, are all wrong for each other. I know you think the only reason I'm down on one knee right now is because of the loyalty I have for your father.

"You're wrong. I'm down on one knee right now because you are the strongest woman I have ever met. You are determined, honest, beautiful, and, yes, a little naive. You are every bit as strong as your father was. I might not make the perfect husband. In fact, I know I won't. But I want to spend the rest of my life falling in love with you."

He pulls a box out of his pocket. He pops it open, revealing a gorgeous princess cut diamond. "Princess, will you marry me?"

I bite my lip as I look into his intense eyes. I have no idea what to say.

Yes.

No.

I don't know.

They all go through my head. And then they all zoom out again. None of them is the right answer. None of them will make either of us happy. None of them will bring an end to this story.

I finally open my mouth to say the only word that feels right leaving my lips, "Maybe."

A slow smile tugs at his lips as he shakes his head at me. "That's not going to work. I can't take that as a yes. I need to hear you say it."

I take a slow deep breath as I tuck a loose strand of hair behind my ear. I open my mouth to tell him my answer when our phones simultaneously go off. I pull my phone out from my clutch.

Mother, the screen reads.

I see Killian reaching into his pocket. He runs his hand through his hair.

We both press accept at the same time. We each lift the phone to our ears at the same time. We both say, "Hello?" at the same time.

We both feel the pain at the same time.

18

───────

"I'll call a car to take us," Killian says immediately, dropping his question.

Now that there are more pressing issues to deal with, it doesn't matter if I say yes or no. His perfect proposal is ruined. Maybe that's a good thing because I'm not sure I had the strength to tell him no, even when it's what is best for both of us.

I watch as Killian talks on the phone as he paces back and forth in the beautiful garden. I...I don't move. I don't know how to feel. It doesn't feel as bad as the last time I got a call like this. It doesn't hurt nearly as much, but it still hurts. Maybe because Granddad is just in the hospital and not dead. Maybe it's because my father was my everything. Maybe it's because, this time, I might have a chance to say goodbye, if that is what this comes to.

I watch as Killian quickly makes his way around the room, blowing out all the candles. I don't move though. I can't. I feel him grab ahold of my hand, but I still don't move. I'm not even sure if I'm breathing or if my heart is still beating.

"Kinsley, we need to go out front. The car should be here any minute."

I still don't move. Killian puts his arm around my shoulders and guides me forward. I move but only because his arm is around me. It takes a long time to make our way through the casino and back out onto the strip. Neither of us speaks as we move. We just move as one unit.

When Killian pushes the doors open to the vibrant lights of the busy strip, I move. I don't know if it's the lights or what that jolts me back to reality. Whatever it is, I'm thankful.

I see the blacked-out Cadillac Escalade parked in front of the casino. I grab Killian's hand. "Come on," I say as I run to the car. Killian runs with me.

I pull the door open and dive into the car as quickly as possible. Killian has already run around to the other side and is jumping in. I close the door and hear a small tear of my dress from getting it caught in the door. I pick up the torn fabric and run it back and forth between my fingers. The fairy tale is over. I glance to my left where Killian sits. This is over.

It hurts to know it's true, but it is. This will wake both of us up. It will make both of us want to live a full life—a life we choose, full of happiness and mistakes, a life we live for us.

Killian closes his eyes when he sees it in my eyes. This is over. He knows it as well as I do.

I tell the driver which hospital Granddad's at, and then we are driving away from the casino, away from my life, away from the fairy tale, and back to reality.

———

"Mom," I say to the blond woman slumped over in a waiting room chair.

Her hair is a mess. It's ratted and dirty. I don't know when she showered last. She's wearing an old T-shirt of Dad's and pink pajama pants. She at least had enough sense to put on tennis shoes.

"Mom," I say again as I grab her shoulders while I squat in my dress in front of her.

She moans but doesn't look up at me. I grab her cheeks, lifting her head. The smell of alcohol is intense on her breath. I have to look away from her to take a deep breath.

Shit, why did she have to do this today?

I have no idea how to deal with her while she's drunk. Dad was always the one who dealt with her when she was drunk. I never had to. Now that she's a raging alcoholic every other night, I don't know what to do. I feel guilty for not taking better care of her, for not staying at home and being there for her. But I thought it was for the best. I thought her therapist and AA sponsor would handle her. I thought she would be better by now.

We never got along, even before it happened, even before I destroyed the family reputation. We never got along when she was sober. We have never gotten along.

"Here," Killian says.

I look over my shoulder and take the coffee out of his hand.

"Have her drink it. It will help."

"Mom." I place the cup in her hand. I wait until she has a good grip on the cup before I remove my hand. "Drink this."

She does. I sit in the chair next to her and take a deep breath for the first time since she called me. How she managed that call, I don't know. I don't know how she did it in the state she is in.

I look up and mouth, *Thanks.*

Killian nods his head as a nurse runs up to us. I stand, afraid she is here to tell us bad news.

"Are you relatives of Lee Felton?"

Killian and I both nod.

The woman sighs. "Good, I need someone to fill out the insurance forms."

My eyes grow wide. I can't deal with this shit, not right now. I need to take care of my mother. I need to see my grandfather. I don't need to be worried about figuring out what insurance he has.

"I'll do it," Killian says, to my surprise. He leans over and softly kisses me on the cheek before he begins following the nurse.

"Wait. How is he doing?" I ask the nurse.

"He's still in surgery. But I'll have someone come to get you as soon as the surgery is over."

I nod and then sit back in the chair next to my mom. I don't know if Killian will be able to fill out the forms. But I have faith he will find a way to keep the nurse away for a little while at least.

I glance over at my mom, who is now sitting up a little higher in her chair. I watch as she runs her hand through her long locks and then sips on her coffee. It seems to be helping.

I shake my head, disgusted that she is drunk. I never imagined she would fall to this level. She seems so lost without my dad. But I know that's not true. She never really loved my dad. She only married him for the money, for the house, to pass on wealth to me. I realize now, looking back on their relationship, they were never happy together. They never loved each other. They never chose each other.

"I'm not drunk," my mother says, glaring at me.

"I never said you were."

She smiles slyly. "You're disgusted. That's what you thought. I'm not drunk. I've only had two drinks."

"Then, why do you look like complete shit? I know it's not because you gave two shits about my father. And you sure as hell don't care about what happens to Granddad."

"Wow, someone has finally grown a pair." She takes a sip of her coffee before staring off into space.

I think the conversation is over, that this is all I'm going to get from her. She's drunk. There is no other word to describe her state.

"I loved your father very much, more than even he knew."

"You don't need to lie to me. Granddad told me. He told me the truth—the only reason you got married was because it benefited the company and your pocketbook."

Her eyes meet mine, but I don't expect to see the pain in them.

"You have no idea what you are talking about. I loved your father very much. Yes, our marriage was arranged, but it was arranged because I loved him, and it was the only way to get your father to notice me instead of being stuck in his career. The opportunity arose, and I took it."

She takes a deep breath. "Don't you dare accuse me of not loving your father. I gave up everything for that man. I never wanted children. Did he tell you that? I never, ever wanted fucking children. But I had one for him. He wanted children, someone to pass on his precious company to. So, I had one.

"I wanted to move out of this godforsaken place. I

wanted to move somewhere with a beach, but I never did. I stayed with your father, even when he stayed late, night after night at hotel after hotel blaming it on work. I knew what he was doing. I loved him, even when he didn't love me back."

Tears are streaming down her face. "I loved him, even when he loved other women." A sob escapes, and she takes a minute to just let it out of her whole body.

"Don't you dare accuse me of not loving that man. I loved him desperately and without asking for love in return. It tears me apart to think that one of the only remaining links I have left to that love might be dying on the operating table." She glares at me. "And the other is about to make the biggest mistake of her life."

I take a deep breath, trying to take it all in, but it's a lot to take in. She accused my father of not loving her, of cheating on her. I don't want to think about it. I've always loved my father. I don't want to know if what she said is true. I can't know.

"What do you mean, I'm about to make the biggest mistake of my life? I thought I already did that five years ago."

She laughs. "What you did wasn't a mistake. I know I told you time after time it was. I know I blamed you for my failed marriage. I blamed you because it was easier to blame you than myself. It wasn't your fault. It was mine. I should never have agreed to marry your father. It was the worst mistake of my life. I ruined my life forever when I said, 'I do.' I can't get back the last twenty-five years. They are gone. I don't even know if I can figure out how to live again for another twenty-five years."

She stands from her chair, surprisingly steady on her

feet. "Don't make my mistake. Don't marry that boy. I'd pull the trigger before I made that decision again."

My mother scares me with her words. I've never heard her talk like this.

I watch her walk toward the restroom, and then I stand and follow her. I'm afraid to leave her alone after she basically told me I should kill myself rather than marry Killian.

I stand outside the restroom as I text Scarlett. I ask her to meet us at the hospital. I tell her I'm worried about my mother's mental state and I need someone to stay with her twenty-four/seven for a while. I know I will owe Scarlett big time for doing this for me, but I don't care. It will be worth it. There is no way in hell I can spend the next few days watching my mother.

I'm not sure I believe a word out of my mother's mouth. I never have. Our relationship is too far gone to be repaired.

When Scarlett texts she will be here in the next half hour, I sigh in relief. I just have to watch my mother for a half hour. Then, I can move on to more important things. Then, I can go back to praying like hell that my grandfather lives.

19

───────

I FEEL a hand on my shoulder.

"I brought you some coffee and breakfast."

I rub my eyes before glancing up at Killian. I take the coffee and breakfast sandwich he brought me before I glance back to my grandfather's hospital bed. He made it through the open-heart surgery, but he still hasn't opened his eyes yet.

I unwrap the sandwich and find a bacon and egg sandwich. I take a bite, letting the greasy goodness dissolve in my mouth. I glance at the clock on my phone. It's seven a.m. We've been here all night.

"You should go home, Killian. You need to get some rest. You've been a great help, but there is nothing else you can do. We have to wait until he wakes up."

He shakes his head. "I'm not going anywhere."

I sigh and take another bite of my food.

Killian has been amazing. He was able to fill out the insurance information without any help. He helped get my mother into Scarlett's car last night. He kept me fed all night. He found some clothes from the gift shop so I could change out of the ballgown I had been wearing. He found me a blanket and pillow, so I could get some sleep. He's been by my side the entire night—taking care of me, holding my hand, doing anything I needed without ever asking what I needed. He just knew. He knew better than I did.

I don't ask him again to leave. In fact, I like having him here.

Killian sits down next to me and unwraps his own sandwich. We eat in silence. Both of our eyes stayed glued on my grandfather, looking for any signs of movement or for any signs he is still in there.

When I'm done eating, I toss my wrapper into the trash can beside the bed. That's when I realize what will make Killian leave. I realize what will make him go back to bed or to work or to wherever he feels he belongs instead of wasting his time in a hospital room.

I slowly turn to face Killian. I don't look sad. I don't look happy. I don't look like anything. "I have an answer for you."

I watch as his eyes fill with regret and pain, a face I wasn't expecting.

"I don't want to hear it, not until after your grandfather wakes up."

"My answer isn't going to change though. Even after he wakes up, I'm still going to have the same answer for you."

"Maybe, maybe not. Either way, I can't hear it until after he wakes up."

I sigh. "Okay." I don't feel okay though.

I need to stop pretending Killian is my future. I need to stop relying on him. I need to stop relying on anyone but myself. I need to be able to make a decision about my life and then deal with the consequences, no matter how awful they are.

I turn back to my grandfather. His eyes open. They open wide.

"Granddad," I sigh as I stand. I embrace his body in a hug.

"Hi, princess," he breathes into my ear as his arm comes around me.

When he releases me, we both turn and stare at Killian.

Terror flashes over Killian's face as he realizes, at any second, I will give him my answer. But he shouldn't seem so afraid. He'll want to hear my answer. My answer will set him free.

"I'll let the nurses know he's awake," Killian says, leaving the room.

I laugh softly at his reaction.

I wait until the nurses and doctors check Granddad over. I wait until after they tell me he should make a full recovery in a few days. A week, they guessed. Then, he will have to frequently meet with a cardiologist for a while, but he seems to be out of the woods for now. I wait until Killian leaves to call everyone at the office to let them know Granddad is okay. I wait until Granddad sits up and seems comfortable. I wait until he is alone. I wait until I'll explode if I wait any longer.

"I'm not going to marry him. I refuse. I'm not going to let you or Dad or Mom or anyone else choose for me anymore. I've made mistakes in my past, yes. I will always regret those mistakes, but I haven't been living since I let you guys control me. Since Dad's death, I've tried to make my own decisions. They haven't always been the best, but I've made them for me."

I pause, giving him a chance to yell at me or tell me I'm wrong.

He doesn't, so I continue, "I can find my own husband

on my own time. I don't need your help. I don't need the money either. I might have a useless degree I don't care about, thanks to you, but I'm smart. I can go back and get my MBA. I can go back and get any degree I want. I can make something of myself on my own. I don't care if I have to live in a box and eat cereal for years until I have enough money to buy a place. But it will be *my* place. It will be *my* money."

I take a deep breath. "I refuse to turn into my mother. I refuse to be that miserable. I won't marry him," I say, collapsing into a chair. Standing up to Granddad took everything out of me.

I look at my grandfather who has yet to say a word. Instead, he is just sitting there with a serious look on his face. It probably isn't fair to him to spring all of this on him, only hours after he woke up from open-heart surgery, but I don't care. I can't live without making my own decisions. I can't keep living like a princess. I have to find my own way in life.

He pats the side of the bed, and I slowly, cautiously get out of my chair and sit on the edge of his bed.

"You're just like your father."

I stare at him in confusion.

I loved my father. He was an amazing man, but I'm nothing like him. He was strong where I'm weak. He was decisive where I'm indecisive. He was a workaholic where I'm lost.

I shake my head. "I'm not."

A smile tugs at Granddad's lips. "You are. You won't listen to anyone. You choose your own path. And you defy my every decision, just like him."

"I never—"

He puts his hand up, stopping me from arguing with

him. "I always thought you would fight me till the very end on my decision for you to marry Killian. I don't think I ever thought you would follow my command. Maybe, if your father were still alive, you would have listened better to him, but I doubt it. Somehow, I think we would have ended up here, both at odds and neither of us wanting to give in."

My head drops. He's not going to back down. I'm going to have to find my way on my own with no money.

"Lucky for you, a heart attack changes an old man like me."

My face lifts as I try to decide if he is serious or not.

His face looks sad. "I didn't listen to your father when he pleaded with me to let him choose his own wife. I thought I knew better." He rubs his neck. "I'm not sure if the company benefited greatly from their union. I know he was never happy in his marriage."

He sighs. "I can't change your dad's fate, but I can give you a chance. I know you have been trying to prove you are worthy of running the company."

I nod.

"You've failed horribly."

I frown but don't deny it. It's true. I'm not the right person to run the company.

"I am willing to give you a chance though."

My eyes brighten just a little.

"Since I promoted Killian to CEO, there is a spot open in the company. We will need a new VP of Operations. I've been looking around, but I haven't found anyone worthwhile yet. Tony obviously isn't a good choice."

I nod, willing him to say the words I want him to voice.

"I'll give you the job."

My hands go around him, tightly holding him, before he

even has a chance to say the rest. He pushes me back up after I've finished smothering him.

"Now, the job comes with some conditions. You will attend business classes."

I nod. I already planned on doing that.

"You will run every decision by either Killian or me."

I nod, not liking that as much, but I'll accept it —for now.

"Lastly, this is a trial run. If you last a year, it can be a permanent position, but Killian or I can fire you for any reason at any time."

I take a deep breath and nod. His terms seem fair, considering I have never run a company like this before.

"If you last a year, I'll give you all of my equity."

I raise an eyebrow at him. "That would be..."

He nods. "You would have controlling power over the company. You would have fifty-one percent. Killian will only have forty-nine."

I take a deep breath, trying to calm my nerves. I can't believe what he is offering me. I don't understand what changed since the heart attack, but whatever it is, I'll take it.

"Do we have an agreement?"

I smile. "Yes."

I extend my hand, and we shake on it.

"Now that, that is taken care of, what is that boy still doing here?"

"What do you mean?"

"I figured, since you aren't wearing a ring and you finally got the balls to tell me you aren't marrying him, no matter what, it meant you told him no."

I nervously twist my strands of hair in front of my body.

"Kinsley?"

"I haven't answered him yet. I tried to earlier, but he wouldn't let me."

"Then, answer me this. How do you feel about that boy?"

"What do you mean?"

He rolls his eyes at me. "Do you love him? And don't you dare lie to me. I've been through enough these last few days. You wouldn't want to give me another heart attack because you lied to me."

I shake my head at his dramatics. I don't know how to answer him because I'm not sure how I feel.

"Maybe. I don't know," I say, getting up from the bed and pacing the room.

He doesn't rush me or ask me any further questions. He just watches me pace and encourages me with his patience to tell him.

"He makes me feel warm when he's around me. I ache when he's gone. He challenges me. He frustrates me."

I walk to the other side of the room.

"He charming, intelligent, strong. He's taken care of me more than he should."

I pace again.

"He was willing to marry me for no other reason than because he felt he made a promise to my father."

I pace again.

"He's decisive and opinionated and so controlling that it pisses me off."

I pace.

"He's serious. He hardly ever laughs. It's annoying really."

I pace.

"He sucks at blackjack and poker. He sucks at all card games."

I stop.

"You love him," he says.

I shrug as tears well in my eyes. "It doesn't matter if I love him. It only matters if he loves me."

And I already know the answer. He doesn't.

Granddad holds his arms out to me. I walk over to his bedside and curl up like a child would in her mother's lap. I let the tears fall as he gently rubs my back until no more tears can fall.

"I'm going to tell you a story I promised I never would."

I hiccup.

He smiles and kisses the top of my head. "It was three years ago. Your father had fallen ill."

I sit up before turning to look at him. "What do you mean, my father was ill?"

He sighs. "You were in school. It was stage one colon cancer."

"What?"

"Calm down. They were able to easily cure it because they'd caught it so early. We didn't want to worry you since there was nothing to worry about. He wouldn't have died from the cancer."

I nod although it doesn't make me feel any better they kept secrets from me.

"Anyway, the cancer scare was enough for your father to rethink his life plans. He loved his work. He loved running the company. It's all he'd ever dreamed about, but it made him realize he wanted more. He wanted to retire, to travel, to find out what living was like, outside of the daily grind of work."

I nod.

"At the time, Killian was aware of what we wanted him to do. He had worked for a few months in the VP position and was doing better than any of us had expected." He pauses. "So, your dad offered him the CEO position with no strings attached."

"You mean, he could have had the position without marrying me?"

He nods. "Yes. He told Killian to think about it, but he wanted an answer soon. Killian went to see you shortly after that."

"I remember. He broke Eli and me up just to spite us, just because he could."

"Is that what he told you?"

"He didn't have to. I understood."

Granddad shakes his head. "He needed to see you. He realized he would be making a decision not only for himself, but also for you, too. He saw how unhappy you were with Eli. Well, I don't really know what else he saw when he went to see you. All I know is, when he came back, he told your father he wasn't ready to take the CEO job yet. He said he wanted to keep the condition that he would have to marry you in order to get it."

I suck in a breath. That can't be true. He wouldn't have come up with a plan so that we wouldn't have to marry— except that he did...to give me a choice about my future.

"Your father realized shortly afterward that he wasn't ready to retire yet. And they never spoke of it again."

"Why would he do that?"

"Oh, sweetie. Isn't it obvious?"

I think for a minute before nodding because it is obvious. There is only one explanation for it.

20

"You're still here," I say when I exit my grandfather's hospital room.

Killian is sitting in a plastic chair in the waiting room. He's still wearing a tux. He must not have found any gift shop clothes that fit him.

"I told you I would stay," he says, standing and putting his phone back into his pocket. "How's he doing?" He nods toward my grandfather's room.

"Granddad is doing well. He's a pretty tough old man... although his heart might have just grown a little softer."

Killian raises his eyebrows but doesn't ask about it, and I don't say anything else about my grandfather.

Instead, I walk to Killian until my lips are just a breath from his, until my body is trembling again, just like it was the last time our bodies were this close to each other. I close my eyes and try to calm my body, but it doesn't work. I open them again and am faced with his intense dark eyes transfixed on mine.

"Ask me," I breathe onto his lips.

I watch him suck in a breath, but he doesn't say anything.

"Ask me," I say again.

"Princess, will you marry me?"

He doesn't get down on one knee. He doesn't pull the ring box still tucked in his pocket back out. He's already decided he knows the answer.

I smile because he's mostly right. "No," I say.

His eyes close, immediately blocking me off. His breathing returns. His head drops.

"Now, answer a question for me."

He takes a deep breath before opening his eyes. "Yes, princess?"

"You have to promise to be completely honest."

"I will," he says.

My heart is racing much too fast. My shaking has increased instead of slowed. My eyes try to close, but I force them to stay open, to stay on him to read his reaction.

I let one more beat of my heartbeat before I ask, "Do you love me?"

A smug grin forms on his face as he takes a couple of seconds longer to answer me than I anticipated. I was wrong. Him deciding to marry me, no matter what, didn't mean what I thought it did. It's part of some other master plan that I don't know about.

"Maybe," he says the word as innocently as I have countless times to him before. His smug smile grows larger.

I can't help the smile that forms on my lips. "I'll take that as a yes."

I launch my lips onto his. It's been too long since I tasted him, too long since he wrapped his arms around me, like he is doing now, too long since I felt truly loved by someone since my father died.

The kiss is more than a kiss. It's a declaration of love, a promise of what could be. It's a chance, a chance to be together because of our choices and no one else's.

He tries to break away from the kiss when my hands start tugging at the hem of his shirt. "Princess, I love your enthusiasm, but we can't do that here. People are watching."

I smile larger though as I grab ahold of his hand and pull him down the hallway. An old episode of *Friends* pops into my head as we make our way through the hospital.

I pass a dark looking room. No nurses are hovering around. I peek through the cracked door. It's empty.

I tug on Killian's arm, and he follows me into the room. I shut the door behind us, and my lips attack his again as my hand pulls at the hem of his shirt. It's then I realize I don't need his shirt off. It's his pants I should be working on.

I grab at the button. It unbuttons quickly, and then I'm unzipping his pants.

He smiles against my lips. "God, if I had known what kind of crazy woman you would turn into when I told you maybe I loved you, I would have told you sooner."

"Shut up, and help me get these pants off of you."

He laughs but complies, and his pants fall to the floor. He grabs my ass and pushes me against the wall.

I moan as his lips touch my neck, and his hand finds my breast.

"This is going to be quick," he says into my neck.

I nod. "Yes, quick," I say. I'm barely able to speak.

I feel him smiling again as he reaches his hand into the front of my pants, cupping my pussy.

"Fuck, Killian!" I scream.

He clamps his hand over my mouth, silencing me. "You can't scream. You can't moan. You have to be silent."

I nod my head, agreeing.

He tugs my pants down, and I feel them fall to the floor.

He rubs his hard cock at my entrance. "God, you're so wet already, baby."

"Please, I need you now," I whisper.

He rubs his cock one more time over my clit before he lifts my legs and thrusts inside me in one motion. I bite my lip to keep from screaming out his name. When I look at him, I can tell he is doing the same. He doesn't hesitate though. He thrusts quickly in and out of me.

God, I want to moan. I want to scream. I want to have him fuck me like this over and over again.

But something does escape his lips when his cock is buried deep inside me with his beautiful eyes locked on mine. "I love you, princess."

He thrusts again, keeping me from responding the way I want to. He thrusts again, building us closer.

"I love you, too," I moan a little louder than I should.

It's then that I realize I forgot one little part of that *Friends* episode. They get caught.

The door opens, and the lights flash on. I glance up, and we both laugh as a young nurse stares at Killian's bare ass. We both laugh as she closes the door and runs away in embarrassment.

Killian starts thrusting again.

"What are you doing?"

He shrugs. "Might as well finish."

I try to catch my breath as I pull my pants back up. I watch as Killian buttons his pants. The nurse has yet to come back, but that's probably because she has called security by now.

Killian doesn't seem to care about getting thrown out though. He walks to me, putting his hands on my waist. "I love you, Kinsley," he says before softly kissing me on the lips. "I know you're not ready to marry me yet. And that's okay. But can we at least date?"

I laugh. "Maybe."

"Yes," he says sternly, making me laugh again.

"Yes," I say.

He lifts me and spins me around as he kisses me again.

But the spin is ended abruptly. I look to the door, thinking maybe the nurse has come back, but no one's there.

"What is it?" I ask.

"Why aren't you marrying me? I thought that was the only way you could be a part of the company."

I smile. "I told Granddad I didn't care about being a part of the company. I told him I didn't care about the money. I told him I refused to marry such an arrogant ass."

He frowns, making me smile larger.

"I told him I was tired of living my life for other people. I told him I'll be making all the decisions in my life now."

He hugs me again. "That's great. I'm so proud of you, princess." He lets me go. "What are you going to do now?"

"Other than be your girlfriend?"

He nods.

"I'm going to be your new VP of Operations."

He grabs me and lifts me, spinning me around again.

We kiss. We laugh. We fall further in love.

When he puts me down, I know I have made the right decision.

The door swings open again, startling us. Two men in black suits walk through the door. They are not security guards.

"Are you Kinsley Felton?" the man says.

"Yes," I whisper.

Killian wraps his arms around me tighter.

The man walks toward us. He grabs ahold of my arm. "Kinsley Felton, you are under arrest."

I expect him to say, for having sex in a spare hospital bed. But that doesn't make sense.

He finishes his sentence, "For money laundering and fraud."

I stare at him, wide-eyed. I have no idea what he is talking about.

Killian is still holding on to my waist, refusing to let me go.

"I'm going to have to ask you to let her go."

Killian does reluctantly, and the man puts the cuffs on me. The man begins walking me out of the room. I hear Killian running next to us.

"Excellent job, Agent Byrne," the man who has me in cuffs says.

I turn to my right to face the direction where the man is talking, but I have no idea who he is talking to. All I see is Killian. Killian *Browne*.

Killian's eyes grow heavy, sad, as he looks from me and then to the man who has me in cuffs. "Thank you, Agent Phillips," Killian says weakly.

My mouth drops. Killian isn't Killian. He's not a CEO. He's a cop or with the FBI or CIA or whatever the hell agents work with.

I force myself to keep my eyes off of Killian or whatever the hell his name is as the man leads me out of the hospital and into the back of a blacked-out Suburban.

I was wrong. I'm always wrong. Killian doesn't love me.

He doesn't care about being a CEO. He was just doing his job.

I try to push Killian out of my head. I try to focus on whatever I'm facing as the car speeds off, leaving the hospital behind. I can't help it though. I glance back at him. Killian's standing on the street, staring at me with an intense stare on his face.

I hate him, I think.

But I don't. The lingering love is still there. I still feel his warm cum pooling between my thighs. I still feel his love even if it didn't exist.

I turn away from him.

Any normal woman would be afraid. Being arrested is most people's worst nightmare. It should be mine, except this isn't the first time I've made a mistake. It feels just like the last time. The pain from being betrayed by a man I thought loved me is the same.

The only difference is, last time I knew what the mistake was. But, this time, I have no clue.

The End

Thank you for reading Maybe Yes! Want to read more of Kinsley & Killian's story? Find out what happens next in>>>Maybe Never & Maybe Always

Keep reading for a sneak peek of Maybe Never...

Sign up to get notified when my new books release and get a FREE ebook here>>>EllaMiles.com/freebooks

Want to order signed paperbacks? Visit:
store.ellamiles.com

MAYBE NEVER PREVIEW

Will one mistake destroy her life? Will one secret? One lie?

Kinsley Felton thought she had found a solution to her problems. She thought she had convinced her family that she is strong enough to run the company, if not on her own, then with help. She thought she had won when she decided not to marry Killian and instead just date him. But everything she thought was wrong.

Killian isn't who she thought he was. Now she is sitting in a jail cell for something she didn't do because of him. But maybe she deserves to sit in jail anyway to pay for her past mistakes. All she knows is she needs to stay far away from Killian no matter how much her heart aches for him.

Will Kinsley let herself get lost in the deceit or will she save herself and take another chance at love?

Continue on to preview...

I pace back and forth in the holding cell, unable to sit patiently like the rest of my cellmates. One woman lies back on one of the benches, seemingly asleep, while another sits across from her, picking the nail polish off her fingers.

Not me though. I can't sit. Not when I have no idea why I'm here. So, instead, I pace back and forth in the small cell, hoping that, soon, someone will come to tell me what the hell is going on. I also have to pee, which is keeping me from sitting down, but I'm not going to go in the toilet in the corner of the room—at least not until I can't hold it any longer.

I think back to the last time I was here. It was the same jail and the same holding cell with the same disgusting yellow walls. Last time, I was calmer, much calmer, because I had accepted that I deserved to be in prison. I had confessed.

I stop pacing when the woman lying on the bench snores, startling me. I don't know why I'm back in jail now. *What did I do?* The agent mentioned something about fraud and money laundering. I didn't do either of those things. It must be a mistake.

And Killian...

I can barely even let my heart go there. One day—actually, less than a day, more like one hour, was all I got with Killian. It's all the time I got to think about a possible future with him.

I thought I loved him.

I thought he was the one for me.

I was wrong.

Killian isn't Killian. Killian is a liar. I chose wrong, again.

I glance at the clock that is barely visible outside the holding cell. It's past midnight. They won't question me tonight. I won't be arraigned tonight. They won't do anything with me tonight. I'm stuck here, in this cold room, with two strange women.

I take a seat on the only remaining bench in the room and rest my head against the wall. I cross my arms over my chest and rub my hands over them, trying to warm up, but I'm still shivering, despite my efforts. I push the urge to pee along with thoughts of why I'm in here out of my head. I push Killian out of my head until the only thing that remains is last time.

This feels just like last time when I had fallen for a man who wasn't what he seemed. Then, I fell again for the wrong man. Even though my father and grandfather had handpicked him, they picked wrong. Maybe there isn't a man out there for me.

I should have learned my lesson the first time. Instead, I'm back in this cell again, and this time, I don't know when I'll be getting out.

Continue reading Kinsley & Killian's story in Maybe Never!

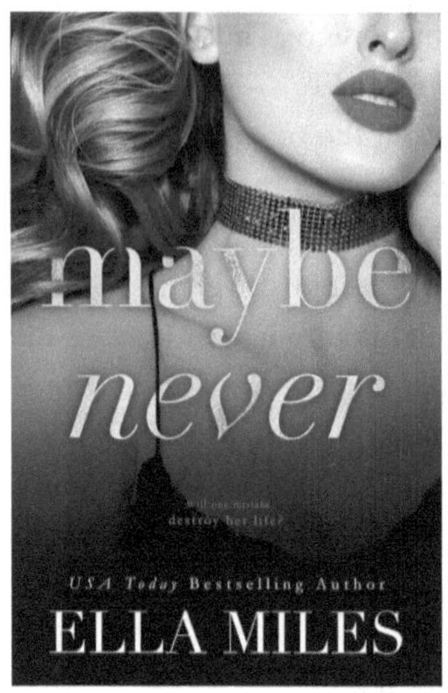

FREE BOOKS

Read **Not Sorry** for **FREE**! And sign up to get my latest releases, updates, and more goodies here→EllaMiles.com/freebooks

Follow me on BookBub to get notified of my new releases and recommendations here→Follow on BookBub Here

Join Ella's Bellas FB group for giveaways and FUN→Join Ella's Bellas Here

Want to order signed paperbacks? Visit:
store.ellamiles.com

ALSO BY ELLA MILES

MAYBE, DEFINITELY SERIES:

Maybe Yes

Maybe Never

Maybe Always

Definitely Yes

Definitely No

Definitely Forever

STOLEN EMPIRE SERIES (Coming 2019):

Taken by Lies

Betrayed by Truths

Trapped by Lies

Stolen by Truths

Possessed by Lies

Consumed by Truths

DIRTY SERIES:

Dirty Beginning

Dirty Obsession

Dirty Addiction

Dirty Revenge

ALIGNED SERIES:

Aligned: Volume 1 (Free Series Starter)

Aligned: Volume 2

Aligned: Volume 3

Aligned: Volume 4

Aligned: The Complete Series Boxset

UNFORGIVABLE SERIES:

Heart of a Thief

Heart of a Liar

Heart of a Prick

Unforgivable: The Complete Series Boxset

STANDALONES:

Pretend I'm Yours

Finding Perfect

Savage Love

Too Much

Not Sorry

ABOUT THE AUTHOR

Ella Miles writes steamy romance, including everything from dark suspense romance that will leave you on the edge of your seat to contemporary romance that will leave you laughing out loud or crying. Most importantly, she wants you to feel everything her characters feel as you read.

Ella is currently living her own happily ever after near the Rocky Mountains with her high school sweetheart husband. Her heart is also taken by her goofy five year old black lab who is scared of everything, including her own shadow.

Ella is a USA Today Bestselling Author & Top 50 Bestselling Author.

Stalk Ella at:
www.ellamiles.com
ella@ellamiles.com